TRAVELLING BACKWARDS

Toby Forward

First published in Great Britain in 1992
by Andersen Press Limited
This Large Print edition published by
AudioGO Ltd
by arrangement with
Andersen Press Ltd 2011

ISBN: 978 1405 664325

British Library Cataloguing in Publication Data

For Charles and Nigel

Printed and bound in Great Britain by
MPG Books Group Limited

ONE

Everyone spoke very quietly, and when Lizzie asked a question in a big voice they all said, 'Sshhh!'

There was Aunty Clara, who sniffed; Uncle George and Aunty Nell who always interrupted each other; cousin Crawly, who was Uncle George and Aunty Nell's son and who was really called Crawford but it was such a silly name and he was such a crawly person that it seemed a waste not to call him Crawly; and, of course, there were Lizzie's mother and father and Gilbert the dog.

'I only asked,' repeated Lizzie in what she hoped was a quieter voice.

'Sssh,' said Crawly.

Aunty Clara sniffed.

'It doesn't matter what you asked,' said Uncle George, 'it's . . .'

'. . . the way you ask it that's so wrong,' continued Aunty Nell. 'You always . . .'

'. . . speak so loudly,' Uncle George

finished.

'She should think more about other people,' said Crawly.

Lizzie hated the self-satisfied smirk on his face when he said this and she promised herself that she would get him for it.

'That's a good boy,' said Aunty Nell.

Aunty Clara sniffed.

Aunty Nell carried on. 'Crawford's always so . . .'

'. . . considerate,' said Uncle George. 'He thinks . . .'

'. . . about other people's . . .' said Aunty Nell.

'. . . feelings,' Uncle George concluded.

'Well,' admitted Crawly. 'I try to be kind.'

Lizzie tried not to be sick. She looked at her mother for help.

'Lizzie does her best,' her mother said. 'She's a good girl, too. But she doesn't understand.'

Gilbert burrowed his wet nose against Lizzie's thigh. She rather thought that he was deliberately wiping his nose against her because dogs don't have handkerchiefs. She looked down secretly and there was a slimy, silver streak on her leg.

Gilbert grinned up at her, his pink tongue flopping out of the side of his friendly face. Lizzie decided it wasn't his fault and she wouldn't get back at him as well. She reached down and ruffled the fur round his neck. Gilbert snuggled up closer and Lizzie felt very pleased to have him there. She smiled down at him.

'Look,' said Crawly. 'Lizzie's laughing. Grandpa's really poorly and Lizzie's laughing at it.'

Aunty Clara sniffed.

Lizzie gripped the fur at Gilbert's neck and promised herself, cross her heart and hope to die, that she would smash Crawly up as soon as they were on their own.

'Not a laughing matter,' said Uncle George. 'It's very . . .'

'. . . serious,' said Aunty Nell. 'That's why we've come all this way, to . . .'

'. . . see Grandpa,' said Uncle George, 'before he . . .'

Aunty Clara sniffed.

'Dies,' said Crawly.

Gilbert shivered and drew even closer to Lizzie.

'That's enough, Crawfy!' snapped Lizzie's mother.

'Don't you speak to ...' said Uncle George.

'... him like that,' said Aunty Nell.

'Sniff!'

Lizzie's lip trembled and a tear splashed down her face.

'Waah!' complained Crawly. 'She shouted at me.'

Gilbert turned to Crawly and growled.

The door opened and Lizzie's father looked in.

'What on earth's going on?' he asked. 'This is a terrible noise. Don't you know that Grandpa's ...?'

'Yes,' said Lizzie's mother quickly. 'You shouldn't leave him alone upstairs.'

'He wants to see Lizzie,' he said.

There was a sudden silence.

Lizzie shivered.

'Do you want to go up and see him?' asked her mother.

4

Lizzie nodded. She couldn't speak. There was something in her throat that was a mixture of sadness and fear, and she was frightened they would hear it if she said anything.

'Come on,' said her father. Lizzie ran over to him and clutched his large hand with her small one.

'And please,' he said to the others, 'try to keep the noise down.'

He closed the door, but not quickly enough to miss the sound of Aunty Clara's feelings.

'Sniff!'

*   *   *

It was bright and warm on the stairs. The sun splattered patterns against the creamy paper on the walls. It was a cheerful, summer day. But Lizzie was cold and lonely, following her father up the stairs. He paused halfway up.

'You'll have to speak quietly to him,' he warned Lizzie.

Lizzie nodded.

'It's not your fault,' said her father with a smile, 'but you do have a very loud voice.'

Lizzie agreed silently.

'You mustn't disturb him.'

'Is Grandpa dying?' Lizzie whispered.

Her father looked very serious.

'I think he is,' he said. 'He's very old and frail.'

'I don't think I want him to die.'

'Sometimes it's best,' said her father. 'When it's the right time.'

'How do you know,' she asked, 'when the right time is?'

Her father looked rather upset and lost for an answer.

'Is it when you're very old?'

'Yes.'

'Fifty?'

'Er.'

'Eighty?'

'Well.'

'Ninety? A hundred?'

'It's different for different people,' he said.

'So how do we know when it's right for Grandpa?'

'I don't know,' admitted her father. 'I'm really not sure.'

'So he might not die?' she asked.

'Sssh! Not so loud.'

'Sorry,' Lizzie whispered. 'Does he want to die?'

'I think you'd better just see him,' said her father. 'But don't talk about dying. Please?'

'Of course not.'

They reached the door and Lizzie's father held it open.

Lizzie had never been so frightened in her life. She squeezed her father's hand.

'It's all right,' he whispered. 'I'm with you. Come on in.'

Grandpa looked very small under the bed covers, smaller than Lizzie. His eyes were closed. She was relieved. If he was asleep they could look at him and then go out. She wouldn't have to worry about talking about whether he was going to die. She wouldn't have to think about what it would be like for him to be dead.

'He's asleep,' she whispered, in a very, very small voice indeed. 'Let's leave him.'

Grandpa's eyes flicked open.

'Hello, Lizzie,' he said. 'Leave us

7

alone, Jack. I want a quiet talk with Lizzie.'

'I'll wait just outside,' he said and closed the door. 'Remember what I said.'

Lizzie nodded. She could be good. She would show them all, Uncle George and Aunty Nell, and rotten Crawly and Aunty Clara. She wouldn't tell Grandpa he was dying.

'I'm dying,' said Grandpa. 'I want to talk to you about it.'

TWO

'No, you're not, Grandpa,' said Lizzie.

'Oh, yes, I am,' he answered. 'Don't you think I know? All these relatives turning up like this. Why couldn't they wait till I'm good and dead? Then they could all come to the funeral and I wouldn't have to see them.'

Lizzie did not know what to say.

Grandpa grinned.

'They're a crowd of freaks, aren't they?'

Lizzie grinned back and nodded.

'Sniffy Clara,' he said. 'She's there. Why doesn't she stop it? When she was your age she used to wipe her nose on her sleeve all the time. Did you know that?'

Lizzie giggled. 'No.'

'Well, I'm telling you. She did. Looked like a snail had crawled up it, silver streaks everywhere.'

'She doesn't wipe it on her sleeve now,' said Lizzie.

'No. Sniffs all the time, though.'

'Yes.'

'And gormless George. I've never known anyone so stupid. If you said "Good morning" to him he was lost for an answer. He deserves that wife of his. They're as bad as each other.'

This was so exactly what Lizzie thought that she did not dare to say anything.

'They're all expecting something in my will,' he said. 'Do you know what a will is?'

'No,' admitted Lizzie.

'A will,' said Grandpa, 'is where you say what you want them to do with your money when you're dead. They've all come round to make sure I haven't forgotten them. Well, I haven't. Do you know what I'm doing?'

'No.'

'I'm leaving Sniffy Clara a box of fifty handkerchiefs.' He cackled. 'What do you think of that?'

'She'll be very cross,' said Lizzie.

'Good,' Grandpa laughed. 'I want her to be. I want her to be cross. And Gormless George. I'm leaving him a dictionary, so he can look up some words and finish off his own sentences.'

'Oh, dear,' said Lizzie. 'He'll be cross too.'

Grandpa laughed even more.

'What about Crawl—Crawford?' Lizzie asked, correcting herself just in time.

'That boy! I can't stand him. He gives me the creeps.'

Lizzie laughed.

'What's the matter?' demanded Grandpa.

'Creeps,' said Lizzie. 'I call him Crawly.'

They both laughed. Grandpa put out his wrinkled, brown old hand and laid it on Lizzie's.

'Oh,' he gasped. 'Creepy Crawly. I'd forgotten him. I hadn't left him anything at all. Should I?'

'I don't know. I don't know anything about wills.'

'You will,' he said, mysteriously, his face suddenly becoming solemn. 'You'll know all about them soon enough. And you mustn't mind what anyone says when you do find out. Do you understand?'

11

Lizzie didn't understand, but she agreed so she nodded.

Grandpa sank back into the pillows, his face suddenly white and pained. His breath came in gasps.

'Worn myself out,' he panted. 'All that laughing. Still, it was worth it, just to see you.' He gripped her hand tightly in his. 'It always cheers me up, seeing you.'

Lizzie felt the tears coming again.

'I love you, Grandpa,' she whispered.

He smiled at her, unable to catch enough breath to answer, but she knew he understood.

'Do you want to die?' she asked.

He shook his head.

'I don't want you to die,' she said. 'You're fun. I want you to stay.'

Grandpa shook his head again.

The door opened and Lizzie's father looked in.

'Everything all right?' He saw Grandpa lying back and came over quickly.

'You've excited him,' he said. 'You'd better leave him for a while. Let him get better.'

Lizzie bent down and kissed Grandpa. He squeezed her hand again, his eyes wet.

Lizzie ran down the stairs and out of the house. Gilbert, who had been waiting for her, leaped through the door before she slammed it shut.

'Well!' complained Uncle George. 'What a way . . .'

'. . . to carry on,' said Aunty Nell.

'Oh, be quiet!' snapped Lizzie's mother. 'Can't you see she's upset?'

'Sniff,' commented Aunty Clara.

*   *   *

Lizzie ran down the road as fast as she could, stopping only when her side hurt and she could run no further.

Gilbert leaped up at her.

'Oh, dear,' she said. Her face was wet with tears and she was sniffing.

Gilbert licked her.

'And I haven't got a handkerchief. I'll be as bad as Sniffy Clara.'

Her breath came in short gasps, as Grandpa's had. But a few moments were enough to let her recover, then

13

she was ready to walk on again.

She made her way straight to a small house, set far back from the road in an overgrown garden. It was masked by a huge hedge that hid it completely.

Although the garden was wild and disorderly it never looked scrubby or uncared-for. There were weeds, but they had not run all over the garden like an army; they lived side by side with real flowers and with fruit trees and shrubs and bushes. There was a herb border where thyme and rosemary, and seven different varieties of sage, and basil and chives all lived and jostled for space with nettles and docks and groundsel and plantain, but they seemed to enjoy each other's company.

The house itself was low and broad, with wide windows and a small door, and eaves that jutted far out over the walls, so low on one side that Lizzie could reach up and touch the tips of her fingers on the jagged edge of the blue slates.

She turned the old-fashioned latch and stuck her head round the door.

'Mrs May!' she called out. 'It's Lizzie.'

Gilbert woofed to show that he was there too.

'Come on in. Come on in,' a voice sang out.

'Do you want any errands?' asked Lizzie when she arrived in the kitchen.

Mrs May lived in the kitchen. It was such a queer house that it did not seem odd that she should. Not that there was no room to live anywhere else. Lizzie could never work out how the house was arranged or where all the space came from. The rooms were all small, but there were lots of them. Too many for the house, it seemed. Lizzie had once tried to walk around the house to see it from the back, so that she could work out where all the rooms could be fitted in, but the garden was so overgrown that she could not find her way around from either direction.

But the kitchen was such a lovely room that Lizzie did not blame Mrs May for living in it.

There was a huge cooker that kept it warm in the winter, and the red tiled

15

floor made it cool in the summer. The ceiling was low and supported by a thick, black beam.

'No, thank you, dear. Not today. I've everything I need.'

'Oh,' said Lizzie. 'Nothing at all?'

'Nothing. But I was just going to have a cup of tea and a biscuit. You'll stay and have one with me, won't you?'

'I'll make it,' said Lizzie. And she busied herself with kettle and teapot and biscuit barrel, while Mrs May sat in silence and watched her.

This made Lizzie feel uncomfortable, because usually Mrs May was very talkative. That was why Lizzie had come here, to take her mind off Grandpa by listening to her.

When she finally sat with a glass of milk and a biscuit Lizzie wished she hadn't come. Mrs May still just looked at her.

'Are you going to tell me?' she asked.

'Tell you what?' said Lizzie.

'Whatever it is that you're upset about.'

Lizzie kicked her toe along the line of the edges of the tiles.

16

Mrs May threw a biscuit to Gilbert. He caught it in his mouth very neatly, then crunched it between his teeth, spilling crumbs on the floor. Lizzie and Mrs May watched him. He licked up the crumbs until the floor was quite clean, the tiles glowing a deeper red than their neighbours where his tongue had licked them.

'You don't have to tell me,' said Mrs May. 'I dare say it's none of my business. I'm just a nosy old woman. That's what happens when you get old. You have to take an interest in other people because there's nothing in your own life to be interested in.'

'You're not old,' said Lizzie quickly.

'Not old,' laughed Mrs May. 'I should say I am. Look at me.'

'Old people die,' said Lizzie.

'Everyone dies,' said Mrs May, quietly. 'Not just old people.'

'You don't look old. How old are you?' asked Lizzie.

It was silly, really, because Lizzie knew that Mrs May was old. Her face was wrinkled in just the way that Grandpa's was. Her hands were old

17

hands. Her hair was grey. But she was quick in her movements, and she was strong—Lizzie had seen her lift pans of boiling fruit to make jam, and Mrs May could knead dough with a ferocity that Lizzie could never manage.

'Oh,' said Mrs May. 'I'm old, all right.'

'How old?'

'Let me see. I remember the war.'

'Which war?'

'All sorts of wars. There was the First World War. I remember that. And others. And the old queen. I remember her. Victoria. And other queens and other kings. And I remember when there were no street lights outside, just gas lamps. And horses and carriages. Those were the days. Before all these cars. Oh, I remember before there were any trains. That was a time. People took days and weeks to get to places.'

Lizzie had heard this before. She loved to hear Mrs May talk about old times. She had used to like to hear Grandpa do it too, when he had been well. But she knew that there was something wrong. Her father had told her that no one remembered before the trains came. The trains had been around for over a hundred years.

'You can't remember that,' said Lizzie. 'You'd have to be nearly two hundred years old. No one's two hundred years old.'

'If you say so, dear,' said Mrs May. 'It's all the same to me.'

'How old are you, then?' asked Lizzie.

'I'm not rightly sure.'

Lizzie flicked her head so that her long, yellow fringe fell away from her eyes and she could look Mrs May clearly in the face.

'Everyone knows how old they are,' she objected.

'There you go again,' said Mrs May. 'You and your everyone. I don't know.' She sipped her tea noisily.

Gilbert, hoping for another biscuit, rubbed himself against Mrs May's legs.

'Look at Gilbert,' said Mrs May. 'How old is he?'

'Three,' said Lizzie.

'That's twenty-one,' said Mrs May.

'You have to count seven years of a dog's life for every one year of a person's life. Give or take.'

'Yes,' agreed Lizzie.

'So, there you are. You can be as old as you're supposed to be. You think you're older than Gilbert, but really he's older than you. You think I'm younger than your grandpa, but really, I'm older than he is. It depends on how you count.'

'I don't understand,' said Lizzie.

'You ask me how old I am,' said Mrs May, patiently.

'Yes.'

'Now, we'll forget that it's a rude question.'

Lizzie, who blushed very easily, went a deep red.

'No. I mean it. You didn't mean it to be rude. Have another biscuit. So, I don't mind answering it. But I don't want to tell you a lie, or confuse you.'

Lizzie could not imagine being more confused than she was.

'So, you see, in a sense, I'm an old person. I'm a lot older than your grandpa, as I said. But in another

20

sense, I'm not as old as I'm going to be. Do you see?'

'No. No, I really don't see.'

'How old is old?' asked Mrs May, with a smile.

'Sixty,' suggested Lizzie. 'I don't know. Eighty; that's really old. Ninety.'

'Twenty?' asked Mrs May.

Now twenty sounded quite old to Lizzie, but she knew it wasn't. It was just grown up, which is supposed to be different.

'No,' she said, firmly. 'Twenty isn't old.'

'But poor old Gilbert will be dead long before he's twenty,' said Mrs May. 'He'll be old at ten.'

'But he's only a dog,' Lizzie argued.

Gilbert whimpered. He put his head to one side and looked at Lizzie out of the corner of his eye.

'Quite right, Gilbert,' said Mrs May. 'Only a dog, indeed. I never heard the like.'

The funny thing about Mrs May was that Lizzie never minded what she said. Uncle George and Aunty Nell could say things that were quite kind, really,

21

but they sounded like tellings off. But even when Mrs May said something that might have been fierce or disappointed she said it in a way that made Lizzie feel it wasn't meant unkindly. So she smiled at Mrs May.

'You know what I mean,' she said. And she knew that Mrs May really did know.

'That's the point,' she said. 'Old is only old when it's old. Old is when it's time to go.'

'Die?'

'Yes.'

'But Grandpa isn't ready to die.'

'Are you sure?'

'Yes. I asked him today. He told me.'

Mrs May pursed her lips. 'Well.'

'I wish we could do something.'

'We can. But I'm not sure it's right.'

'Oh, please,' begged Lizzie. 'Please do something. Can you? Can you really?'

She looked at Mrs May with wide eyes and her mouth slightly open so that her tongue peeped out. Gilbert waited for an answer.

THREE

Mrs May stood up, and Lizzie noticed how quickly she moved for an old lady, and how confidently.

'I'm sorry,' she said. 'If I've been rude. I didn't mean to.'

'Bless you,' said Mrs May. 'You've not been rude. Whyever do you say that? You're just upset about your grandpa. Well, we'll do something about that.'

She opened the door of a huge cupboard that was built into the wall of the kitchen. Inside were rows and rows of bottles.

'Elderberry, no. Elderflower, no, but I'll take a bottle of that out for later. Dandelion, nettle, carrot, no, no, no. I know it's here, somewhere.'

The bottles clinked. The sunlight struck them and bounced back, purple and red and blue and yellow and green.

'Right at the back,' said Mrs May. 'It's always the way when you're looking for things, isn't it?'

23

She seized the bottle she was looking for, drew it out and carried it to the big kitchen table.

'There,' she said.

It was hardly what Lizzie would call a bottle at all. The glass was so thick and rough that it looked more like glazed pottery. And it was a dark green, like the pebbles on the bottom of a stream when weed has grown in it. Lizzie thought it had something of the same shifting, uncertain quality of a stream; the surface shimmered, confusing her eyes. It was shaped like a small goldfish bowl with a tall neck. At the top it was sealed with red wax over what Lizzie guessed must be a cork.

'Now,' said Mrs May, very firmly. 'I really shouldn't be doing this. I can't think why I am. I suppose it's because I like you. And I don't like to see you so upset. But that isn't a good enough reason. All the same, I'll probably do it. Tell me,' she fixed Lizzie with a hard stare. 'Tell me what you want for your grandpa.'

Lizzie swallowed.

'I don't want him to die,' she said,

clearly. 'Not yet.'

'When?' demanded Mrs May.

'Oh, I don't know.'

'Sorry. I shouldn't have interrupted. Tell me in your own way. I want to be sure.'

'I just don't want him to die. I want to have him here for longer. He's always been such fun, someone I could talk to, play with. I want that. I don't want him in bed all the time, like he is now. I want him well again.'

'That'll do,' agreed Mrs May. 'That's all I wanted to hear. Except,' she added, 'how long do you want him for?'

'For ever, of course,' said Lizzie. Her voice was croaky and she was brushing her sleeve over her eyes.

'I don't know about that,' Mrs May said, quietly. 'Only a few of us are around that long. All the same—' She opened a knife and cracked the red wax from round the lip of the strange bottle. Then she twisted a corkscrew into it and drew the cork.

'Ah,' she breathed.

The low room filled with a delicious scent. It was the smell of fields when

25

the rain first falls on them, releasing their richness; the smell of gardens in the early morning; the smell of leaves, rotting underfoot, when you walk through a deep wood; the smell of hay being scythed; the smell of herbs; the smell of a spade cutting through the earth.

Mrs May pushed the cork halfway back in. The scent faded a little but remained as a presence in the room.

'One small glass every day,' she said. 'Until he's better. No more. And bring back what you don't use.'

'I will.'

'And on no account must you drink even the smallest drop yourself.'

'I promise,' agreed Lizzie. 'I'll let you know if it works.'

'Oh,' smiled Mrs May, 'it'll work. That's not what you've got to be frightened of. Here.'

Lizzie took the bottle from her. 'Careful, Gilbert,' she warned as the dog leaped around her. 'You'll make me drop it.'

'Remember,' called Mrs May, as Lizzie disappeared. 'You got what you asked for.'

*　　　*　　　*

'You're in trouble,' shouted Crawly when he saw Lizzie arrive back at the house.

He was swinging on the garden gate, and his weight made it squeak in protest.

CREAK.

'What's that you've got?' he asked pointing to the bottle.

'Nothing.' Lizzie pushed it behind her.

'Let's see.'

'No.'

'You're in trouble,' he said again.

Lizzie looked him up and down, trying to think of an insult.

'You're as fat as your mum,' she said.

Crawly's jaw dropped.

'Don't you talk like that,' he shouted. 'We aren't fat.'

'Not fat!' Lizzie was astonished. She had never thought about it before just this moment, but now that she had said it it was clearly the truest thing she had

27

ever heard.

'Of course you're fat. You're all fat.'

CREAK.

'We're not.' Crawly puffed out his cheeks in anger and looked fatter than ever.

'Look,' said Lizzie fairly, because she had forgotten that it had been an insult, now she wanted to explain the truth to Crawly. 'You're all fat. It probably isn't your fault. I mean, your mum probably married your dad because he was fat, or the other way round, of course,' she added generously, not liking to blame one party more than the other. 'And then when they had you, you just had to be fat. Stands to reason. Like two black dogs always have black puppies.'

'WE ARE NOT FAT!' screamed Crawly.

'But your dad wobbles,' Lizzie pointed out. 'Not as much as your mum, but quite a lot.'

'You shut up!' said Crawly.

Gilbert bounced round him, jumping up at the gate and sending it swinging violently. And as the gate moved,

28

Crawly wobbled.

CREAK.

'Look!' said Lizzie helpfully. 'You're doing it now.'

'Lizzie! Is that you?' called her mother. 'You're late.'

'You're in trouble,' shrieked Crawly, wobbling with fury. 'You've missed your dinner. And you've upset Grandpa.'

'I have not!' Lizzie said, pushing her small face up to Crawly's fat one.

'You have. It was ages ago. We've ate ours.'

'Not that,' she said. 'I don't care about that. Grandpa. I never upset him. It's you he can't stand.'

'Come on in, dear,' said her mother. 'I've got you a sandwich. Lunch was hours ago. Yours is spoiled.'

Lizzie went through the gate and swung it shut behind her as hard as she could. Crawly flew round, trapped his fingers in the gap, fell off, bumped his head and howled.

'She shouldn't be eating ...' said Uncle George.

'... those sandwiches,' said Aunty

29

Nell. 'She should be sent . . .'

'. . . to her room without any . . .' said Uncle George.

'. . . dinner,' said Aunty Nell.

'Sniff,' Aunt Clara contributed to the telling off.

'I'm really not hungry,' said Lizzie. 'Can I go and see Grandpa?'

'Did you ever hear . . .' said Uncle George.

'. . . the like of it?' asked Aunty Nell.

'Upsetting Grandpa fit to . . .'

'. . . kill him,' they said.

'How dare you?' demanded Lizzie. 'How dare you say such a thing to me?'

'That'll do, Elizabeth,' said her mother, using her proper name so that she would know it was serious.

'That poor old man,' said Uncle George. 'He needs . . .'

'. . . peace and quiet,' said Aunty Nell. 'So that he can die in . . .'

'Get better,' interrupted Uncle George. 'So he can get better.' He glared at his wife. 'He needs rest, and quiet and nursing so that he can get better,' he said, finishing a whole sentence for the very first time Lizzie could remember.

Aunty Nell's cheeks wobbled with embarrassment.

'You want him to die!' shouted Lizzie. 'That's what you're here for. So that he'll remember to leave his money to you when he dies. Well, he won't, because he's not going to die. I won't let him. Not for Sniffy Clara, or Gormless George or any of you.'

'Lizzie!' said her mother, who was so shocked that she could not even remember to call her by her you're-in-trouble-now-my-girl name.

'Oh, I don't care,' said Lizzie. 'I'm going to see Grandpa.'

Aunty Clara was so shocked that she forgot to sniff and a drop of water gathered on the tip of her nose. It hung there, trembling, till it tickled her, then she dragged an offended sleeve across her nose, leaving a silver streak.

'She should be taken to her . . .' said Uncle George.

'. . . room, and given a good . . .' said Aunty Nell.

'. . . hiding!' snapped Aunty Clara, glaring at them all. 'She should be given a good hiding.'

'Oh, be quiet, all of you,' said Lizzie's mother. 'She's right, isn't she? That's what you want. That's what you're here for.'

*   *   *

Lizzie let herself into Grandpa's room without knocking.

At first, she thought he was dead already, he was so still and white.

She crept over to the bed. He was breathing very gently.

Lizzie pulled the cork from the bottle with a small 'plop'.

In the dark bedroom the scent seemed more intense than ever, as though she could smell the fields and woods on the day the earth was made.

Grandpa opened his eyes but he did not see her. He was looking far beyond Lizzie into a place that she could not see. She stroked his hand and he struggled to fix his eyes on her.

'You're all right, Grandpa,' she whispered. 'I've brought something to make you better.'

He smiled, but shook his head.

'Too late,' he whispered.

Lizzie poured some of the liquid into a glass by the side of his bed. It was deep green, yet it shone with a light of its own. She raised the glass to his lips and moistened them with the elixir.

Grandpa took a deep breath. He licked his tongue on the lip of the glass. Lizzie tilted it further. The liquid slipped through his lips and he swallowed, a little at first, then more, then all of it. He sank back into the pillows.

Lizzie recorked the bottle and put it into the cupboard next to his bed.

'Don't go, Grandpa,' she said. 'Not yet. I'm not ready for you to go yet.'

She fancied that he was breathing more peacefully, that he was drawing deeper, stronger breaths, but perhaps it was only that she wanted him to be better and she imagined it.

Her father was waiting for her when she stepped outside.

'It's your bedroom, I'm afraid,' he said.

'All right,' agreed Lizzie. 'But I won't

apologise to them.'

'You won't come downstairs until you do,' he said calmly.

'Really?' Lizzie's eyes grew wide with amazement. 'Do I really have to apologise? I only told the truth.'

'That's the way it is,' he explained.

'I'll do it now, then,' Lizzie offered. 'But then I'm going to my room. I don't want to see them again today.'

'That seems reasonable,' agreed her father.

'What about Crawly? Do I have to apologise to him, too?'

'Probably not,' he said. 'I think we can forget Crawfy.'

The aunts and uncle heard Lizzie's apology in silence, which Lizzie thought was rude. She did not know that her mother had threatened to turn them out of the house if they said anything else to make Lizzie unhappy.

Later, her father brought her some scrambled egg to her room and then he sat with her and played cards.

'You can go downstairs,' she offered. 'I don't mind being up here on my own.'

'No,' he decided. 'I think I'll stay, if you don't mind.'

The sound of Uncle George and Aunty Nell interrupting each other drifted up the stairs, with Aunty Clara's sniff contributing its say from time to time. Lizzie looked at her father and nodded.

'Your deal,' she said.

Later, she slept badly, dreaming that she could hear noises of someone walking about in Grandpa's room, and she dreamed that her own room, the whole house in fact, was filled with the wonderful smell from the green bottle. She heard an owl hoot, and a cat squawl; a dog barked and something tiny scurried past her behind the skirting board; the tree outside her bedroom window stroked its branches across the glass. She was awake when the first ribbons of light fluttered across the sky and the birds began to sing, but then she fell into a deep sleep and was confused and startled, over an hour later, by the loud knocking at her door.

'Breakfast,' called a voice. 'Rise and

shine. Don't let the grass grow beneath your feet.'

Lizzie sat up with a start.

The door flew open.

'Have I got to drag you out of bed?' He stuck his head round the door. 'Or will you get up yourself?'

Lizzie screamed.

'Grandpa!'

FOUR

'Never felt better,' said Grandpa, dancing into Lizzie's bedroom.

Lizzie jumped out of bed and hurled herself at him.

'Grandpa,' she shouted again, unable to think of anything else to say.

'Will you stop that noise?' demanded her father's angry voice. 'Don't you know that Grandpa's very ill?'

Grandpa dodged quickly behind the door. Lizzie's father pushed it wide open and stood in the doorway.

'Look, Lizzie,' he said in a stern voice. 'I really don't want to start another day by getting angry with you. Not after yesterday. But you really must remember how loud your voice is, and that your grandfather is . . .'

'Boo!' shouted Grandpa, leaping out.

In his rumpled nightshirt, and with his grey hair sticking up like an unmown lawn, Grandpa looked a strange sight, but it was the suddenness of his appearance, not its peculiarity

37

which shocked Lizzie's father and made him jump with a strangled cry in his throat.

'Aaaghr!' he screamed.

'He he,' laughed Grandpa. 'Gave you a shock, didn't it? Eh? He he!'

Lizzie's father gaped at him and tried to speak.

'Grrrr,' he gurgled.

'Grrrr, yourself,' Grandpa growled in return.

Gilbert pushed a wet black nose through the door.

'Grrrrr,' he joined in.

Lizzie laughed.

'Grandpa,' gasped Lizzie's father. 'You should be in bed.'

'In bed! In bed!' he shouted. 'It's morning. You don't lie in bed in the morning.'

Other faces joined Gilbert in the doorway, attracted by all the noise.

'Ssh,' said Uncle George, 'you'll wake . . .'

'. . . up Grandpa,' said Aunty Nell.

'Booo!' said Grandpa again, and he laughed even louder when he saw their astonished faces.

'Oh, dear me,' he wheezed. 'I can see this is going to be a good day.'

'What's going on?' asked Aunty Clara. 'I thought I heard Grandpa's voice.'

'You did,' said Grandpa, 'and you're going to hear a lot more of it. For a long time.'

Aunty Clara sniffed, disapprovingly. 'But I thought you,' she began.

'That is,' said Uncle George.

'What we wanted to say,' said Aunty Nell.

'You thought I was dead!' said Grandpa. 'Or very nearly. Dying, anyway. Well, I ain't. Not going to. Not for years.'

'What's this funny smell?' said Crawly, who was still half asleep and hadn't seen Grandpa. 'Like someone mowing a lawn.'

'Morning, Crawly,' Grandpa sang out.

'Crawfy,' snapped Aunty Nell. 'His name's . . .'

'Crawly!' said Grandpa. 'Ha! I got you that time, didn't I? I finished it first. Creepy Crawly. That's who that is. Come on, Lizzie. Breakfast. I feel as

39

though I haven't eaten for years. Let's get some bacon, and eggs, and tomatoes.'

Lizzie ran out of her bedroom after him.

'And black pudding,' he said. 'I love a bit of black pudding for breakfast.'

Uncle George looked at Aunty Nell. Aunty Nell looked at Aunty Clara. Aunty Clara looked at the open door. And Lizzie's father looked at all of them.

'And kippers. I must have kippers. And toast. Lots of toast.'

There was a small scream of surprise from Lizzie's mother as the kitchen door opened. Then a shout of joy and the silence that follows when two people hug each other.

Aunty Clara sniffed very loudly and went into the bathroom. Uncle George and Aunty Nell put their heads together and went back to their room, muttering. None of them looked very happy.

Except for Lizzie's father who sat on her bed and smiled and scratched a thoughtful finger down his cheek.

*　　*　　*

In the end, Grandpa had to settle for cereal, boiled egg and toast because Lizzie's mother didn't have kippers or bacon or black pudding or tomatoes.

'Sausages,' suggested Grandpa. 'You must have sausages.'

She shook her head. 'They aren't good for you,' she said.

'He he,' laughed Grandpa. 'I don't care. Look at me. I'm fine. I'm going to live for ever.'

And Lizzie's mother did look at Grandpa, and she agreed that he looked better than he had for years, even before he became ill.

'Look,' he said. And he pushed his chair back and sprang to his feet and started to jump up and down.

'Yes,' agreed Lizzie's mother.

Gilbert barked and tried to nip Grandpa's heels when he landed, but Grandpa was too quick for him and he kept on springing away. Gilbert growled playfully, and he barked and snapped, but Grandpa always kept one jump ahead of him. Lizzie laughed until she hurt.

'Cup of tea?' Lizzie's mother offered.

'No. No thanks,' he said. 'I've got something in my room. I'll have a little drink of that while I'm dressing.'

'No,' said Lizzie. 'You mustn't. I've got to take that back to Mrs May.'

'Take it back,' said Grandpa. 'Nonsense. There's lots left. You can take the bottle back when it's empty. Get some more.'

He crossed the room and opened the door.

'No,' insisted Lizzie. 'I've got to take it back. I promised. You mustn't drink any more.'

'Be ready in ten minutes,' Grandpa ordered her as he climbed the stairs. 'We'll go out and have some fun.'

*   *   *

Heads gaped out of the windows when Grandpa and Lizzie set off for their walk.

'Put your head in, Clara,' Grandpa called out, waving his stick at her.

42

'You're showing your curlers to the neighbours.'

SNIFF. SLAM. Aunty Clara's head disappeared.

'Toodle-oo, Crawly,' Grandpa called. 'Don't catch cold.'

Crawly's head popped in.

'Mouths tight shut,' Grandpa advised Uncle George and Aunty Nell. 'You'll trap the flies.'

'Well, I . . .' said Uncle George.

'. . . never did,' finished Aunty Nell. And their window slammed shut as well.

'Whoopee,' he called. 'We're off.'

' 'Bye, Grandpa,' waved Lizzie's father.

'Coming with us?' Grandpa invited him.

'Don't think so. Better stay here. Sort a few things out.'

'Just as you like. Tootle pip.'

Lizzie had to trot along to keep up with Grandpa.

'Where are we going?' she asked, a little breathlessly.

'Out,' said Grandpa. 'About. On the town. Somewhere. Anywhere. Don't care.'

He lifted his walking stick, put it against the railings and ran down the side of the park, dragging it along.

PLINK. PLINK. PLINK. PLINK. PLINK. PLINK. PLINK. PLINK. PLINK. PLINK. PLINK. PLINK. PLINK. PLINK. PLINK. PLINK. PLINK.

Gilbert howled with laughter and jumped up, trying to catch Grandpa's walking stick in his mouth.

'Down, sir. Down,' howled Grandpa.

'Ow, woof, yow,' Gilbert answered him, and they both fell about with laughter.

'Oh, dear me. Oh, dear,' panted Grandpa, helpless with laughter, as Lizzie trotted up to join them.

'You're too fast for me,' she complained.

'Oh, dear,' he gasped. 'Get my breath back. Oh, dear. Haven't run like that for years.'

And it was true. Lizzie had never seen Grandpa run. Ever.

'Must have a sip,' he said. He took the green bottle from his pocket.

'You mustn't,' Lizzie warned him. 'Please. Give it back to me. Mrs May said ...'

'Pooh,' said Grandpa. 'That Mrs May wants it all for herself, whoever she is.' He put his finger along the side of his nose and winked at Gilbert. 'Doesn't she? Eh? She knows a good thing.'

He pulled out the cork and took a deep swig, drawing his sleeve across his mouth when he had finished, then he recorked the bottle quickly and slipped it back into his coat pocket. For those few moments Lizzie felt her head swim as the rich, sweet odour drifted out of the slim neck of the dark bottle. Then it was gone.

'Off we go!' Grandpa called. He waved his stick.

'Oh, please,' said Lizzie. 'Not so fast. I can't keep up.'

'I know,' said Grandpa. 'The car. We'll go for a drive.'

'We can't,' said Lizzie. 'You don't drive.'

'Don't drive! I don't drive!' Grandpa exploded. 'What nonsense. You come along and see. My word. That drink

45

does a bit of good. I've really got my breath back now. Off we go.'

'But where?' said Lizzie.

'To Bill Bowen,' said Grandpa. 'To get the car.'

FIVE

Lizzie had never seen Grandpa drive a car. She supposed he was too old ever to have learned. She had certainly never heard that he might have one of his own.

' 'Course I have,' he said. 'I just haven't felt like driving her for a long time. Bill Bowen looks after her for me. He's a great one for cars, is Bill, always lying underneath one with his face covered in oil and his hands in the engine.'

They turned down a side street and then up a little alleyway, through a narrow tunnel between two houses and found themselves in a courtyard with big black gates and a small black door. A battered sign, with paint peeling from it announced:

BOWEN'S AUTOS

There was a wider driveway out of the courtyard on the other side, but there was no sign of activity or business and there were no cars, no customers.

'Must be his day off,' said Grandpa. 'We'll knock.'

He strode across to the small black door and rapped on it with his stick.

Gilbert barked impatiently.

'There's no one here,' said Lizzie.

Grandpa knocked again, almost breaking through the door with the strength of his rapping.

'All right. All right,' came a wavering voice. 'I can hear you. Hold your horses. I ain't so quick, these days.' All through this complaint there was a rattling of keys and chains. 'Hold on. I can hear you.' CLANK.

'Come on, Bill Bowen. We haven't got all day.'

At last, the door drew open and a small, wrinkled face peered through the gap. 'Who is it?'

'Jack,' said Grandpa.

Bill Bowen's face creased up in concentration.

'Jack Blake,' said Grandpa impatiently. 'Open up.'

The door closed and a chain was

released. It opened up again, fully this time, to reveal a tiny old man. He was stooped forward so that his shoulders looked as though they wanted to touch each other in front of his chest. Except that he didn't seem to have a chest any more, it had sunk away. His clothes had been made for someone else, someone bigger, and they hung loosely on him, except where they had been tightly gathered at the waist by a thick belt.

'I thought he was dead,' said Bill.

Grandpa chortled. 'You look as though you should be,' he said. 'Where's Mabel?'

'In the garage,' said Bill.

'Let's get her out, then.'

'How do I know you're who you say you are?' asked Bill cautiously.

'Look at me,' demanded Grandpa. 'I haven't changed, have I?'

Bill looked him up and down. 'That's the trouble,' he said. 'You haven't. It must be,' he scratched his head, 'ten years.'

'Fifteen,' interrupted Grandpa. 'Fifteen years since I saw you.'

'And you haven't changed,' said Bill. 'So you can't be Jack Blake.'

'Ah,' said Grandpa, knowingly, rubbing his finger along the side of his nose. 'But if I haven't changed, I can't be anyone else, can I?'

Bill screwed his face up in concentration while he worked this out, but in the end he gave up, shrugged his shoulders and said, 'I'll open up for you, then.'

'Who's Mabel?' whispered Lizzie.

'You wait and see,' said Grandpa while Bill fumbled about with a huge bunch of keys.

The big black doors to the garage were stiff and heavy and it took all three of them, with Gilbert yapping at their heels, to drag them open. The shafts of morning sun thrust into a vast, open garage, empty save for a single shape hunched up in a corner underneath a tarpaulin. All the workbenches and shelves were dusty. Clouds of dust rose up from the draught made by the sweeping doors. Moths flew round and round in circles in the bright sun like a swarm of insects.

'There she is,' said Bill.

Grandpa bounded over and dragged the sheet away.

'Oh,' gasped Lizzie. 'She's beautiful.'

Bill looked embarrassed.

'I've kept her clean and nice,' he said. 'Whenever I could. I didn't like to see her go to ruin.'

Grandpa's eyes were wet with tears. He moved closer to Bill and put his arm around him. Bill looked startled at the strength and grip of his old friend.

'You've been good to her, Bill,' said Grandpa. 'I'm grateful.'

'There was nothing else to do,' mumbled Bill.

'I've never seen anything like her,' said Lizzie. 'Except in museums. Can she really drive?'

'Oh, yes,' said Bill. 'I don't just polish her. I run the engine every week, keep it sweet and oiled. I check the tyres. And I take her round the yard every now and then. Not out on the road, though. I couldn't do that. I'm too old. But she'll go, all right. Anywhere you like.'

'Good old Mabel,' said Grandpa.

Lizzie stroked her fingertips across the car's paintwork. The body was deep red and the wings were a rich cream. The chrome of the bumpers and the headlights shone like silver. Inside, the dashboard was a warm mahogany and the seats were leather. Mabel smelled more like a library than like a car.

'Good old Mabel,' said Grandpa. He jumped in the driver's seat and grabbed the rubber bulb of the horn.

PARP!

'YOWL!' added Gilbert.

'Jump in,' Grandpa ordered.

Lizzie stepped on to one of the wide, black running boards that swept down the sides of the car. She turned the gleaming handle, swung open the door and settled herself into the delicious-smelling soft leather of the front seat. Gilbert leaped past her into the back and sat there, his tail thumping against the seat, mouth wide open in a doggy grin, tongue hanging out of the left side of his wide, wet mouth.

PARP! PARP!

'Coming?' Grandpa shouted to Bill

Bowen.

Bill shook his head.

'I'm too old for all that,' he said. 'Couldn't stand the excitement.'

'Brrrr!' laughed Grandpa. 'You're as old as you feel.'

'How old do you feel, then, Jack?'

'Oh, about forty,' said Grandpa.

Lizzie was astonished that he should still feel as old as that. He was behaving like a boy.

'If that,' he added.

GRRRAAAGGH, the engine roared as Grandpa pulled the self-starter.

Mabel juddered and spluttered, then there was a PRAAAP, like a firework going off and she settled down into a steady, if still rather noisy, engine rhythm.

'Wonderful!' yelled Grandpa over the noise as it echoed round the empty space. 'They don't make 'em like this any more. You can hear the power. You can feel it.'

Lizzie could certainly feel and hear something frighteningly powerful coming from beneath Mabel's bonnet and shaking them all pleasantly like a ride at the fair. It was like being in a car for the first time, like understanding for the first time that all that power that made a car go fast had to come from something dangerous and alive.

'We're off!' shouted Grandpa. He shot the gear stick into place, lifted his foot from the clutch, seized the steering wheel, and they were away.

Mabel leaped forward, stopped suddenly, struggled to move again and roared in anger.

'Handbrake,' said Bill. 'Take the handbrake off.'

'Whoops,' said Grandpa. 'Soon get used to her again.'

He slipped the brake, pressed his foot down, more carefully this time and they moved again.

' 'Bye!' he called. ' 'Bye, 'bye!'

Lizzie waved. Gilbert wagged and woofed. Grandpa grabbed the horn again.

PARP!

Bill raised a tired arm and saluted them.

'Take care of her,' he called after

Grandpa. 'Take care.'

'We wiiiiilll,' Grandpa's voice promised, disappearing out of the garage. 'Weeee wiiiiii . . .'

And they were gone.

Bill Bowen looked at the place where Mabel had stood. He picked up the tarpaulin slowly and folded it away.

*   *   *

'Careful,' Lizzie warned in a rather frightened voice. 'You'll kill us.'

'Perfectly safe,' said Grandpa, throwing the car round a corner and screeching away from the courtyard.

BOWEN'S AUTOS

disappeared and they were off.

The road was narrow. A red van came towards them.

'Slow down,' begged Lizzie.

PARP!

'Get out of my way!'

The van driver's face twisted into a spasm of fear.

'You're on the wrong side of the

55

road,' shouted Lizzie.

'Wrong side,' agreed Grandpa, shaking his fist at the van driver. 'Wrong side.'

'Not him! You!' she said.

Mabel plunged forward, straight towards the red van.

PARP!

'Wrong side,' said Lizzie, desperately.

The two vehicles looked each other in the eye, charged forward, then, at the last moment, the van driver swerved away, across the road, up the pavement, round the side of Mabel and slammed on its brakes. Grandpa gave Mabel another spurt. She leaped forward, found her own side of the road, swept round another corner and was gone.

'Attagirl, Mabel,' sang out Grandpa. 'You showed him.'

PARP!

The van driver pulled a huge handkerchief out of his pocket, as red as his van, and mopped it against a face that was as red as the handkerchief.

'Whew,' he said. 'That was close.'

'Wooahah,' screamed Grandpa.

'We're on our way.'

WOOF.

'Slow down, please,' Lizzie asked. 'We'll crash.'

Reluctantly, Grandpa took his foot off the pedal and let Mabel slow down.

They turned again, away from the side streets where Bowen's Autos had its garage, and found the main road out of town.

Even when Grandpa drove carefully, as he did now, heads turned in the street to watch them. People waved as they passed. Mabel told people she was coming well before they could see her, so by the time she was in sight they were ready for her. They cheered when black smoke puffed out of her exhaust and she exclaimed PRAAAP! They laughed when she pulled up at the traffic lights and shook and wobbled, waiting for them to change. They waved happily as she clanked and roared past. And Grandpa waved back at them and smiled and nodded.

Lizzie was very embarrassed at first, but she soon got used to it and rather liked the way everyone wanted to be pleasant to Mabel.

'Where to?' asked Grandpa.

'Oh, I don't mind,' said Lizzie. 'Anywhere.'

'Old Bill's certainly taken care of her,' said Grandpa admiringly. 'She could go anywhere. But where do you want?'

WOOF, said Gilbert and grinned out of the window at a signpost.

TO THE SEASIDE

'That's right,' said Grandpa. 'Always trust a dog. To the seaside.'

'It's a long way,' said Lizzie. 'We'll be very late.'

'Nonsense,' said Grandpa. 'You're with me. You're perfectly safe. Day out at the seaside with your grandpa. Couldn't be better.'

So the road stretched out in front of them as they left the town. The fields took them into their arms. The hills lifted them up and lowered them gently down. Lizzie sat in the front seat and felt the wind lift her hair away from her face and she looked sideways at

Grandpa, seeing his happy smile and his bright eyes and she said a small, silent thank you to Mrs May for the wonderful medicine that had brought him back to her and given her so much fun and happiness with him again after he had been so ill. And the road twisted and wound along until they climbed higher and higher, up the sturdy hills and reached a topmost point from which all suddenly fell away into the blue emptiness of sky and sea.

'Oh,' whispered Lizzie, with a sigh of pleasure. 'We're there.'

'Down the hill and we shall be,' said Grandpa. 'Whheeee!'

WOOF. Gilbert leaned forward and licked Lizzie's neck.

SIX

Mabel gave a wheeze and a sigh and juddered to a halt as Grandpa steered her to the side of the road and turned off the engine.

'Whew,' he said.

WHHEWWW, echoed Mabel.

Lizzie hugged herself in delight and gazed around.

She saw a small bay tucked into the fold of a high, red cliff. From where she sat everything beyond the furthest points of the bay was invisible. It was like being hidden away in a bright, sunlit cave, protected from the rest of the world.

'Look!' she pointed. 'Look at the way the sun is bouncing up off the waves.'

And it was. Tiny points of silver light broke from the tips of the waves and sparkled at them.

'Whew,' Grandpa repeated.

WOOF.

'Shush, Gilbert,' said Lizzie. 'What's the matter, Grandpa?'

Lizzie looked at him closely. He seemed to have more hair than he had yesterday. And it was darker, browner, less grey. And his cheeks were plumper, younger. But his hands were trembling and he was struggling for breath.

'Please,' she said. 'Please. Are you all right?'

Grandpa felt in the pocket of his jacket and pulled out Mrs May's bottle.

'In a second,' he wheezed. 'Just. Just.' He pulled in his breath with difficulty.

Lizzie was frightened. What if something awful should happen? What if he should die, here, with just her and Gilbert?

'Just have a little drink,' he said.

But his hands were trembling too much to open the bottle.

'Please,' he said, turning to Lizzie.

Lizzie drew the cork. The scent of woods and fields seemed stronger every time the bottle was opened. For a second the sea and the sand and the blue sky disappeared and Lizzie seemed to see herself in a thick wood, with branches arched over her head, broad trunks all around her and the sunlight green as it filtered through the flat leaves. Then she blinked and saw Grandpa holding his hand out for the bottle.

He took a deep drink, spilling a little down his chin, and then sighed heavily.

'That's better,' he said. 'Just a little breathless. Long drive. Haven't been out much lately. Not used to it.'

He recorked the bottle and put it away again. Lizzie noticed that there was still a lot of the medicine left.

'I really think we should take it back,' she said.

'Nonsense,' Grandpa objected. 'Non. Sense. Does me good.'

And it did. He leaped out of the car, slammed the door and strode round to let Lizzie and Gilbert out the other side.

'Good old Mabel,' he said, patting her on the bonnet. Mabel's headlights winked back at him in the sunshine. 'Now then. Let's have a look. Where shall we go first?'

'Down to the beach,' said Lizzie, who could hardly wait.

'Mmmmm,' he wondered. 'All right. But you need to swim. Got your cossie?'

But of course, Lizzie did not have her swimming costume.

'I didn't know we were coming,' she said sadly.

' 'Course you didn't. I didn't. No one didn't, er, not,' said Grandpa getting confused with the sentence, but more or less sorting it out by the end. 'We'll get you one. And a towel.'

So it was in a lovely red swimming costume that Lizzie ran down to the sea and leaped into the frilled waves which curled up and threw themselves over her.

'Cold?' asked Grandpa.

'No. Lovely.'

Grandpa threw his stick far out to sea and Gilbert jumped in after it, swam to it and brought it back in his mouth.

Grandpa took off his shoes and socks, rolled up his trouser legs and danced in the shallow water, grabbing his stick and throwing again and again for Gilbert. Lizzie raced the dog, trying to get to the stick first, but although she was a good swimmer the waves threw her back and Gilbert always won. She was soon breathless with laughter and with effort.

'Oh,' she said, throwing herself on the dry sand. 'I'm worn out,'

'Happy?' said Grandpa.

'Ow!' she shouted. A heavy, wet dog landed on her and rolled off, showering sand over them both.

Grandpa ran after Gilbert pretending to beat him with his stick. Gilbert was far too fast and far too twisty for Grandpa.

'Shouldn't be doing that,' said a fat lady in a deckchair.

'Poor dog,' said her friend, who had on a wide hat.

'A old man like him,' said the fat lady.

'Orter know better,' agreed her friend.

Lizzie blushed and turned away, trying not to listen, but it was hopeless.

'Doesn't seem right in the head to me,' said the wide hat.

Gilbert squirmed out of the way of Grandpa's stick, dodged to one side, jumped clear and landed right in front of their deckchairs. A flurry of sand shot up, covering the two women.

'Well, I never,' said the fat one.

'Orter be stopped,' wailed her friend. 'Orter be taken away.'

Lizzie silently begged that Grandpa would go over and apologise and stop the two women.

'Waaah!' he roared.

'Oh,' shrieked the wide hat.

Grandpa danced up and down and patted his hand against his mouth, howling and hooting. 'Ow-ow-ow-ow-ow-ow-ow-ow-ow,' he sang. And he waved his stick at them.

'You stop that,' said the fat one, 'or I'll see about you. Silly old man.'

Lizzie grabbed Grandpa's arm.

'Rock pools,' she said. 'Please. Let's see the rock pools.'

WOOF, said Gilbert and bounded off to the far side of the bay.

'Did you see their faces?' gasped Grandpa. 'Oh, dear. Oh, dear.'

'Didn't orter,' floated after them. 'Reely didn't orter.'

'Should be locked up.'

The rock pools were slippery with

seaweed. Gilbert fell in the biggest one instantly, and Grandpa nearly followed him.

'That was close,' he said, grinning at Lizzie.

'Don't go there,' said a man in green wellingtons.

Lizzie looked round. The man was speaking to a small boy with a net and a blue bucket.

'What you caught?' called Grandpa.

The boy looked at him shyly.

'Over here, Laurie,' said Green Wellingtons.

The boy went away, reluctantly. Grandpa followed.

'Got anything good?' he said.

Laurie turned towards him.

'Careful,' warned Green Wellingtons. 'You'll slip and hurt yourself.'

'He's all right,' said Grandpa. 'Give him a chance.'

'Let's try this one, Laurie,' said the Green Wellingtons, ignoring Grandpa.

Grandpa lifted his arms and looked at them. He took his feet off the rocks, one at a time, balancing dangerously and he stared at them. He opened his jacket and peered down at his body. Laurie watched this in silent fascination.

'Come on, Laurie,' said Green Wellingtons.

But Laurie could not take his eyes off this strange performance and he nearly slipped badly walking backwards.

'Careful!' shouted Green Wellingtons. 'Hi! You!' he called to Grandpa. 'What are you playing about at?'

Grandpa's jaw dropped open and he pretended to be amazed. It was a very bad performance. He turned his head and looked behind him. He looked both ways. He looked up, then down. Then he pointed to himself.

'Me?' he said, at last.

Lizzie was trying so hard not to laugh that her stomach hurt. Laurie was spellbound. Gilbert jumped up at Grandpa and licked his face.

'Yes, you,' said Green Wellingtons. 'You nearly made my son fall over.'

'Me?' repeated Grandpa.

'Yes!'

'Oh, I thought I was invisible. I

67

thought you couldn't see me, couldn't hear me. I wasn't even sure I was here.'

Laurie laughed out loud.

Lizzie squealed.

Green Wellingtons frowned.

'When you didn't answer me,' said Grandpa. 'I thought perhaps I'd become invisible. I just wondered if you'd caught anything?'

'No,' said Laurie. 'I'm not allowed.'

'Come on, Laurie,' said Green Wellingtons.

'I'm not allowed to hang over the sides of the pools,' said Laurie, 'in case I get wet.'

'You're supposed to get wet,' said Grandpa. 'That's what you're here for.'

Green Wellingtons stepped forward quickly to get Laurie away, but he moved too fast, lost his footing and slipped into a deep pool. The water came right over the top of his wellingtons, nearly up to his waist.

WOOF, said Gilbert delightedly. Then he jumped in with him and splashed water all over him.

'Stop!' yelled Green Wellingtons. 'Stop! Mad dog!'

Gilbert enjoyed being shouted at and he leaped about even more.

'Gilbert!' called Lizzie, through her laughter. 'Here, boy!'

Gilbert jumped out. Green Wellingtons followed, much more slowly, making slurping and squelching noises as he lifted himself clear. There was a small crab clinging to the top of his wellington.

'Come on, Laurie,' he ordered. 'We're going.'

Laurie's eyes filled up with tears. Saying nothing, he began to follow his father.

'You can't do that,' said Grandpa.

'Look,' said the man. 'You've caused enough trouble.'

'No, I haven't,' argued Grandpa. 'I didn't push you in. And look, he wants to fish the rock pools. Why should he go just because you're wet?'

Green Wellingtons looked at Laurie who was trying very hard not to cry.

'We'll look after him,' offered Lizzie.

'You can sit on the beach and watch us,' said Grandpa, 'while you get dry.'

Laurie looked up at his father.

Green Wellingtons glowered at Grandpa. SQUELCH. 'It's too dangerous,' he said.

Laurie shrugged, almost smiled goodbye to Lizzie but could not quite make it, then began to walk towards Green Wellingtons.

'No,' said the man. 'You're right. Let him stay. I'll watch you from over there, Laurie,' he pointed.

'I'll see you to the edge of the rocks,' offered Grandpa, and he took the man's arm.

'He's wonderful,' said Laurie quietly.

'He's my grandpa,' said Lizzie.

'Is he always like this?'

'He's always been fun,' said Lizzie. 'But not just like this.'

'He's great.'

'Haven't you got a grandpa?'

Laurie looked sad.

'I did,' he said. 'But he died.'

Lizzie felt funny inside.

'Was he nice?'

Laurie nodded and looked out to sea, away from Lizzie.

'I'm sorry,' she said.

'It's all right,' said Laurie.

70

'My grandpa was very ill,' said Lizzie. 'But then some special medicine made him better. And he can do things now he couldn't do before. Even before he was ill.'

'How?'

Lizzie thought hard but she could not think of an answer. 'Let's fish,' she said.

Gilbert got in the way a lot when they were fishing, so in the end they sent him away to chase sticks. When he was with them he frightened all the fishes and crabs away, but when they were quiet they caught a tiny flatfish, two crabs and a prawn, and a fish, with a big head and fat whiskers, that was almost as big as Lizzie's little finger. Grandpa showed them how to lift stones so that the fish and crabs scuttled about in the bottom of the pools. Lizzie fell in twice and Laurie fell in once. His face went rigid with panic.

'It's all right,' said Grandpa. 'You're only a bit wet. It'll soon dry.'

'Dad'll be cross,' said Laurie, looking towards his father on the beach.

'Don't think so,' said Grandpa. 'How can he be? He fell in himself.'

Green Wellingtons (except he wasn't Green Wellingtons any more because he had taken them off and was drying his toes in the sun) waved to Laurie and laughed. Laurie relaxed.

Grandpa threw his stick out to sea and they all went back to Laurie's father with their catch while Gilbert swam out to retrieve the stick.

'Thank you,' said Laurie's father.

'I'm a bit wet,' apologised Laurie.

'Doesn't matter,' said his father, ruffling Laurie's hair. 'Get as wet as you like. It's the seaside.'

Laurie grinned up at him.

'See the crab,' he said.

'It's a beauty,' agreed his father.

Gilbert landed in the middle of them with a delighted WOOF, and he dropped the stick on Laurie's father.

'Throw it for him, Dad,' said Laurie.

'All right?' he asked Grandpa.

'Be my guest.'

Laurie's father walked out to the water's edge. He lifted the stick above his head, circled his arm and threw it far out to sea. A wave caught it, flicked it over and dragged it further out.

Gilbert dived into the water and chased it.

The stick drifted away from them.

'The tide's turned,' said Laurie's father. 'It'll carry it right away. Sorry.'

'Gilbert!' called Lizzie. She ran down to the water's edge with Laurie. Together they cupped their hands over their mouths. 'Gilbert! Come back! Leave the stick!'

Gilbert swam out. He was a strong swimmer, and the flow of the tide carried him faster and faster away from the shore. As the waves rose his head dipped out of sight, then back again, then out of sight again.

'Gilbert! Come back!'

Laurie's father waded out to sea, getting soaked again, right up to his waist, but the sand shelved quickly and he couldn't go any further.

Gilbert had quite disappeared.

'I'm sorry,' he said, dripping back to them. 'I'm so sorry.'

SEVEN

They waited, with their eyes fixed painfully on the bright sea, long after Gilbert had disappeared.

'Come on,' said Grandpa. 'We can't stay for ever.'

Lizzie looked up at him. 'You're going to,' she said.

Laurie and his father looked puzzled but they said nothing.

'I'll put the fish back,' said Lizzie. 'And the crabs.'

'And the prawn,' added Laurie.

They picked their way carefully across the rocks and emptied the bucket into a big pool. The fishes darted away and were gone immediately. The prawn flicked its tail and snapped out of sight. The smaller crab dug itself into the sand till only its eyes were left. The other crab moved slowly sideways under an overhanging rock.

'At least they're all right,' said Lizzie. She stood on tiptoe, using the extra height of the rocks to help her look out to sea. No sign of Gilbert. More and more rocks were uncovering as the tide sucked out.

'Ice creams?' Laurie's father suggested.

Laurie smiled and nodded. Lizzie nodded.

'That's him,' said the fat lady.

'Orter be locked up,' said wide hat.

Two husbands and a tray of tea sat next to them now.

Grandpa looked at them, then turned away.

'That's right,' said the fat lady. 'Frightened to have a go now, aren't you? Now our husbands are here.'

'Orter be ashamed,' said the wide hat.

Grandpa trudged silently through the sand.

The ice creams were huge and white and pink and green. The four of them sat on a bench looking out to sea, licking.

'Was he your dog?' asked Laurie.

'My very own,' said Lizzie, firmly. 'Mine.'

'He was lovely,' said Laurie's father.

'He is lovely,' said Lizzie. 'He isn't dead. He's lost. He'll come back.'

There was a silence.

'How old, er, is Gilbert?' asked Laurie.

'Twenty-one,' said Lizzie.

'That's old,' said Laurie. 'He didn't look old.'

'For a dog,' said Lizzie. 'Twenty-one for a dog. Three for a person. It's different.'

'Oh,' said Laurie.

'He might not come back,' said Grandpa, gently.

'I know,' agreed Lizzie.

'You see,' said Laurie's father. 'Everything goes away, one day. Clothes, books, food, pictures, animals. Even people.'

'I know,' agreed Lizzie.

'Laurie had a hamster,' he said.

'That's right,' said Laurie. 'Biscuit.'

'Biscuit?' said Lizzie.

'He was called Biscuit. We only had him a week.'

'What happened?'

Laurie sniffed and licked his ice cream. 'Don't know. One morning, he

76

was just dead. He had lots of water, lots of food, lots of straw to sleep in.'

'Oh,' said Lizzie.

'It happens,' said Laurie's father.

'In the morning. I went to look at him, and he was just dead. Curled up in the straw.'

'Everything goes away in the end,' said Laurie's father.

'I know,' said Lizzie. She looked at Grandpa, who had not said anything. 'But I'm not ready for Gilbert to go. Not yet.'

Her ice cream was melting in the sun, and a sweet stream was making her hand wet and sticky. Lizzie licked all round it and looked fiercely out to sea.

'It's time to go,' said Grandpa, at last.

Lizzie and Laurie crunched the bottom of their cones and walked side by side behind Grandpa and Laurie's father.

'You'll look out for him, won't you?' said Lizzie. 'He'll come back.'

'Yes,' said Laurie. 'Gosh, is that yours?'

Mabel looked very pleased to see them. Her silver bumper grinned out at them in the dying sunlight.

'We're back, old girl,' said Grandpa. 'Ready to go home.'

WOOF.

Lizzie squealed.

Gilbert bounded out from behind Mabel, Grandpa's stick in his mouth.

WOOF.

'Where have you been?' screamed Lizzie.

Gilbert jumped up at her, putting wet foot-marks all over her.

Laurie jumped up and down and clutched his father's hand.

Grandpa looked very pleased to see Gilbert, but he muttered, 'Don't understand, really. Can't keep getting things back.'

No one listened to what he was saying.

'He must have swum right out for the stick and come back to one of the tips of the bay where we weren't looking,' said Laurie's father. 'If you think about it, the edge of the bay is a long way out from where we were standing.'

'Is that right, Gilbert? EH? Is it?' demanded Lizzie.

WOOF, said Gilbert, ignoring the question. He dropped Grandpa's stick at his feet, ready for it to be thrown again.

'No, you don't,' said Grandpa. 'No, you don't. Into Mabel, everyone.'

Mabel's sides shook with pleasure. Grandpa squeezed the horn.

PARP!

'Goodbye.'

' 'Byeeee.'

'Safe trip.'

'Enjoy your holiday.'

' 'Bye. 'Bye.'

'Get wet. Really wet.'

'I will.'

WOOF.

PARP!

' 'Bye.'

The fields embraced them again, and the hills lifted them swiftly home. But not before the last fading light of the day had lain down and died. A moon rose over the trees and lit them home with a paler, more reflective glow.

'You're so late,' said Lizzie's mother.

'I can't imagine what you were thinking of,' her father told Grandpa off. 'Keeping Lizzie out so late.'

WOOF.

'Oh, be quiet, Gilbert. This is nothing to do with you. We were so worried,' said her mother.

'Where's Sniffy Clara?' demanded Grandpa.

'Gone,' said Lizzie's mother. 'They've all gone: George, Nell, Clara and Crawly, I mean Crawfy.'

'Well, that's a relief,' said Grandpa.

'They're coming back in a few days,' said Lizzie's father. 'To see how you're getting on.'

'Well, they'll get a shock, won't they? Because I'm fine. And I'm getting better, all the time.'

'But you can't keep Lizzie out like this,' said her mother. 'Stop avoiding it. It isn't safe.'

Grandpa decided not to argue.

'We had a wonderful time,' said Lizzie, hugging them both. 'He's the best grandpa in the world. He took us to the seaside in Mabel. And we swam and looked in rock pools and had ice creams. And Gilbert got lost and then we found him again. And we met a boy called Laurie with a horrid father who was really nice really, when you really got to know him, and he didn't mind you getting wet, especially after his wellingtons got all soaked, and he was really nice really, after all, and . . .'

'. . . and it's time you went to bed,' said her mother. 'Bath first, then straight to sleep.'

'All right,' agreed Lizzie.

'Did you really take Mabel?' asked her father.

'Oh, yes,' said Grandpa. He yawned. 'Do you know. I'm really rather tired myself. I think I'll go to bed too.'

'I didn't know you still had her,' said Lizzie's father. 'After all this time.'

'Oh, yes,' said Grandpa. 'Couldn't get rid of her. How can you get rid of someone you love? Goodnight.'

Lizzie's father went outside to look at Mabel. She stood by the side of the road, quiet and calm, tired perhaps after her long journey. He placed his hand on her smooth bonnet.

'It's a long time, old girl,' he said, 'since you used to take me to the seaside. What's going on? What's happened to Grandpa?'

Mabel smiled up at him.

He looked at the dark sky, the overhanging branches of the trees. A light went on in an upstairs window.

'Good evening,' said a low voice.

Lizzie's father jumped. He had not heard anyone walking down the street towards him.

An elderly lady stood by his side. She was tall, slightly taller than he was, and her eyes were bright and sharp even though her skin was dry and wrinkled.

'Good evening,' he answered.

Her eyes followed his, up to the bedroom window. Grandpa's shadow was cast on the curtain. He raised one arm and put something to his lips and seemed to drink. The tree overhead swayed and creaked, and there was no wind. The night aroma of the garden thickened and grew sweeter.

'A fine evening,' said the lady, without taking her eyes from the lighted window.

'Lovely,' agreed Lizzie's father.

Grandpa lowered his arm.

'I'll bid you goodnight,' she said, and

passed on.

'Goodnight,' he called after her. 'Goodnight.'

* * *

'Lizzie,' said her mother. 'We were very worried.'

'I'm sorry,' said Lizzie. 'I won't do it again.'

Her mother hugged Lizzie.

'It's so strange,' she said. 'Grandpa was so ill. And now I don't understand it.'

'It's lovely,' said Lizzie. 'He's wonderful. I want him here always.'

'Goodnight,' said her mother.

'Goodnight,' said Lizzie.

EIGHT

'I want you to come and see Mrs May,' said Lizzie the next morning.

'Erm, I'm not sure,' said Grandpa. 'I might be busy.'

'You can't be busy,' argued Lizzie's mother. 'What with?'

'Oh, this and that,' Grandpa guessed. 'There's a lot to do. After being poorly. I want to get about.'

'You could get about by going to see Mrs May,' said Lizzie's father.

The breakfast table was a strange sight. Lizzie and her mother sat facing each other, as usual. Gilbert lay under the table with his head poking out in case some food dropped down, as usual. But there were two men there instead of one. Two men, facing each other from the other two sides of the table. Lizzie looked from one to the other and back again, and she could hardly tell which was her grandpa and which was her father.

And no one said anything about it.

That was the strangest part.

Grandpa's hair was thick again where it had grown thin. His bald patch had grown over. The grey had disappeared and it was as deep brown as Lizzie's father's, deeper, perhaps, because he did not even have the streaks of grey at the side.

They looked like twins—father and son, the two Jacks.

And no one had said anything about it.

'Oh, all right,' he agreed. 'I wanted to go out with you, anyway,' he told Lizzie. 'We can see your old woman first.'

He put on a blazer—white with dark blue and gold stripes, and a straw hat with a ribbon in the same colours.

'Haven't worn these for years,' he said.

Lizzie thought he hadn't.

'Won't you be too warm in that?' she asked, hoping he would take it off.

'Not a bit,' he said. 'Just the thing for the summer.' He put his finger along the side of his nose and winked. 'Just the thing for the river,' he said.

'The river?' said Lizzie. 'Are we really?'

'Just you wait.'

WOOF, said Gilbert.

'Take care,' said Lizzie's mother. 'And don't be late, today. I'll have tea ready at five.'

'WOOF,' said Grandpa, taking Gilbert by surprise.

Gilbert ran ahead of them, then stopped, panting, then ran ahead again.

Grandpa waited until they were out of sight of Lizzie's house. 'Do you know Knock-Down-Ginger?' he asked.

'No.'

'Wait here,' he said. 'Pretend to do your shoelace up.'

Lizzie knelt down on the pavement, next to the front wall of a garden. Grandpa went through the gate and walked casually up the path. He rapped on the door with the brass knocker.

RAT-A-TAT-TAT!

Then he sped down the path and swung round past Lizzie.

'RUN!' he ordered.

Lizzie leaped to her feet and sprinted after him. He was too quick for her to catch him.

'I can see you!' shouted an angry voice. 'I know you, Lizzie Blake. I'll tell your mum!'

'Oh, dear, oh, dear,' laughed Grandpa when they were round the next corner.

'You shouldn't have done that,' said Lizzie. 'I'll be in trouble.'

'No, you won't,' promised Grandpa. 'You didn't do anything. You were out with me. I'll tell her you didn't. They won't be able to argue with a grown-up.'

'Where's the bottle?' asked Lizzie, as they walked on. 'Did you bring it with you?'

'Ah,' said Grandpa. 'Ask no questions, you'll hear no lies.'

But Lizzie saw his hand go to his jacket pocket, to check.

'You'll have to give it back,' she said. 'To Mrs May.'

They nearly caught up with Gilbert, but he ran off again as soon as they drew close. Grandpa stepped off the pavement, grabbed a knocker and rapped.

RAT-A-TAT-TAT!

'Run!'

And they were off. Gilbert barked with joy and sprang ahead of them.

'You little perisher! I'll see to you!' shouted an angry voice.

WOOF.

'Stop that,' said Lizzie when they were safe again.

'She ran up the street after us,' laughed Grandpa. 'Did you see her?'

'Yes. And I want you to stop.'

'Spoilsport,' said Grandpa.

Lizzie giggled. 'It was funny,' she admitted.

WOOF.

'You've drunk too much of that stuff,' said Lizzie. 'You shouldn't be like this. You're too young.'

'Too young,' said Grandpa. 'You can't be too young. I've been too old for too long. This is wonderful.'

'But Mrs May only gave it to me to make you better. To stop you . . .'

'Dying,' said Grandpa. 'To stop me dying. And it has. I'm not dying. I'm never going to die.'

Lizzie bit her lip.

'Let's do another one,' said Grandpa.

Lizzie was very firm when she forbade him to.

'Girls,' said Grandpa.

'This is it,' said Lizzie.

They walked up the path, and Grandpa bent down to sniff the herbs. Lizzie lifted the latch. 'Mrs May!' she called out. 'It's Lizzie. Come on,' she said to Grandpa. 'We're going in.'

Grandpa nodded and walked to her, then he grabbed the door, rapped very loudly on it and ran back down the path.

'See you at the river,' he called. 'When you're ready.'

'Grandpa!' shouted Lizzie.

'Hello,' said Mrs May. 'Come on in. Come on in.'

WOOF. Gilbert pushed into the house and Lizzie followed, clenching her fists in anger and embarrassment.

'Come on in,' said Mrs May. 'Goodness, what a noise. You don't need to knock. Come on in.'

'I'm sorry,' said Lizzie.

Mrs May was at the stove, stirring something in a heavy iron pot.

'And you needn't shout,' said Mrs May.

'Sorry,' whispered Lizzie.

'That's better.'

'It was an accident.'

'Rather a noisy one.'

'I mean, I didn't do it.'

'I'll just –' Mrs May tasted the hot liquid in the pot. She pulled a face. 'Ugh,' she said. 'Disgusting. That's just right. I'll leave it to simmer. Now. Have you brought my bottle back?' She looked straight at Lizzie with a challenging stare.

'Oh,' said Lizzie. 'I'm sorry.'

'I said just enough,' said Mrs May, 'to make him better. Not a drop more. Didn't I?'

Lizzie nodded. She bit her lip again and hoped she wouldn't cry.

'And is he better?'

Lizzie nodded.

'And have you brought my bottle?'

Lizzie shook her head.

Mrs May waited for the silent answer to settle in the empty space.

Gilbert, unhappy at the long pause, snuffled round Mrs May's feet.

'I'm sorry,' said Lizzie again.

She looked up and was surprised to see that Mrs May did not look angry, but her voice was still firm when she asked, 'And where is it, now?'

'Grandpa's got it.'

'And is he going to give it back to me?'

'I don't think he wants to. I tried to make him. I brought him here, just now. That was him knocking on the door.'

'Is he waiting outside?'

'No. He ran away.'

'Knock-Down-Ginger,' said Mrs May. 'Do you know it?'

This question made Mrs May smile.

'He might bring it back,' said Lizzie. 'When it's empty. Or if there's only a little left.'

'That bottle will never be empty,' said Mrs May.

'No,' said Lizzie, who thought that she had known that already.

'So,' said Mrs May. 'We must get it back some other way. Will you help?'

'Oh, yes,' said Lizzie.

'At any cost?' Mrs May was still

smiling, but her voice was more firm than ever.

'I suppose so,' agreed Lizzie. 'It depends.'

'At any cost?'

'All right.'

'You'd better find it,' said Mrs May. 'Before it's too late.'

'What will happen when it's too late?'

'Don't even ask,' Mrs May warned her. 'Do you know where he is?'

'At the river.'

'Off you go then.'

Lizzie stayed still.

'Yes?' asked Mrs May.

'I'm sorry,' she said, for a third time.

Mrs May came forward and wrapped her in her arms. 'It's not your fault,' she said. 'It's not even his. It's mine, really. I shouldn't have given it to him.'

'Why did you?'

'You were upset. I don't know. It seemed right at the time. Perhaps it was. We'll see. Go and get the bottle for me.'

Lizzie smiled. 'Thank you.'

'By the way,' asked Mrs May, before Lizzie left. 'How old is he now?'

Lizzie was not very good at knowing how old grown-ups were. 'Still old,' she said. 'Forty? Fifty? Same as Dad, about.'

'All right,' said Mrs May. 'We may be in time. Be quick.'

*   *   *

'Over here!'

Grandpa waved to Lizzie.

WOOF.

Gilbert jumped right away from the bank. His paws touched the side of the punt. His claws scraped against the varnish.

SPLASH!

'Hurrah!' shouted Grandpa. 'Dog overboard!'

WOOF.

Gilbert lunged about in the water, tipping the punt violently as he tried to scramble in.

'Grandpa. Come to the shore,' begged Lizzie.

Grandpa stood up and pushed the pole into the muddy bottom of the river. The punt touched the bank.

Gilbert ran up the grass, leaped again and landed in the middle of the punt, where he shook himself violently and covered Grandpa with spray.

'Get down. Mind my blazer.' Grandpa jumped out of Gilbert's way, but Gilbert was so pleased to see Grandpa that he leaped up and put two big wet pawprints on his striped blazer.

'GRRRRR,' growled Grandpa, but Gilbert enjoyed this even more and jumped up again and gave him two more pawprints.

'Down there, Gilbert,' said Lizzie, climbing aboard. And Gilbert settled down in the front of the punt and hung out a pink tongue like a pennant.

'Oh, this is lovely,' said Lizzie. And she hugged Grandpa and slyly felt the small bottle in his blazer pocket.

'Like it?' he said proudly. 'It'll do us, I think. Are you settled?'

Grandpa pushed off from the bank with his foot, dropped the end of the punt pole into the river and sent them skimming off.

'Wheeee!'

'Be careful,' warned Lizzie.

'You know,' said Grandpa over his shoulder, 'you're always telling people to be careful. You're as bad as a grown-up, you are. No sense of adventure.'

BANG!

The punt had collided with a rowing boat.

'Sorry,' called Grandpa. 'Just getting going.'

'Orter be more careful,' said a lady in a wide hat.

'It's him,' said a fat lady with her.

'What's that?' asked one of the men. There were two of them rowing.

'It's that old fool with the stick and the dog,' said the fat lady.

'Orter be locked up,' said the wide hat.

'Can't be,' said the second man. 'He's not old.'

'That's the dog, though,' said the fat lady.

'And that's that skinny girl with the turned up nose,' said the wide hat.

Lizzie put her tongue out.

'Good girl,' said Grandpa, giving the pole a good shove.

'Sauce!' said the wide hat.

'My old dad told me about you,' said Grandpa, to the disappearing rowing boat.

'You're as bad as what he is,' complained the fat lady.

'Orter be . . .'

The punt turned a bend in the river and they were alone.

WOOF, Gilbert called after them.

'All right, boy. They've gone,' said Grandpa. 'Here, Lizzie, have a look in that bag, will you?'

'Wow,' said Lizzie. 'Cakes, sandwiches, fizzy drink, apples, chocolate, crisps, more chocolate.'

'I like chocolate,' explained Grandpa.

'And pickled onions,' said Lizzie. 'I don't like those.'

'I do,' said Grandpa. 'With the sandwiches.'

'This is lovely,' said Lizzie. She lay back on the cushions and watched Grandpa poling the punt along. It looked very easy.

'Throw me an apple,' said Grandpa. Lizzie tossed one up to him and he took big bites out of it as the punt glided along between strokes.

Woof, complained Gilbert. So Lizzie opened a packet of crisps and he ate them slowly and with great enjoyment.

'Aren't you hot?' asked Lizzie.

'No,' said Grandpa.

'In your blazer, I mean.'

'Not really. Made for the summer, this blazer was. Made for punting in.'

'I just wondered.'

'Thank you.'

SLUUURRRP.

'What was that?' asked Lizzie.

'Pole got stuck. The river's a bit muddy here. Soon get it free.'

Grandpa wrestled with the pole and it came out all of a sudden SPLLLOPP. He staggered backwards, running most of the length of the punt, and very nearly ran off the other end before he could get his balance back.

'Steady on,' called a man from a rowing boat.

WOOF, said Gilbert.

YAP, answered a little white dog.

'Are you all right, sir?' asked a man. There were three of them, all in striped blazers like Grandpa's. One was playing a small banjo, very badly.

97

'Shut up, Montmorency,' he said to the dog.

YAP.

'Never does a thing I tell him,' he said to Lizzie, raising his hat politely.

Lizzie smiled.

WOOF.

'Gilbert!'

YAP.

'Montmorency!'

'Perfectly all right, thank you,' Grandpa answered, as the two boats crossed. 'Been on the river long?'

'Oh, yes,' said the third man. 'Ages.'

'Seems like years,' said the man with the little banjo.

'Goodbye,' called Grandpa.

The boats drifted apart.

'Good day, to you,' the three men sang in chorus. They lifted their hats.

WOOF.

YAP.

The plucking of the banjo faded.

'Please be careful,' said Lizzie.

'There you go again,' laughed Grandpa.

'Perhaps I should take your blazer so that it doesn't get wet,' offered Lizzie.

'The water's going all up your arms when you lift the pole.'

'All right,' agreed Grandpa. 'Not a bad idea. But I'll just have a little drink first. It's thirsty work.'

He took out the little bottle and uncorked it. A kingfisher darted out from the trees, broke the calm water, there was a flurry of wings, then it flew up with a fish gleaming silver in its mouth. The trees bowed down over the water's edge as if in adoration.

'Ah,' said Grandpa. He put the bottle in his trouser pocket, took off his jacket and threw it over to Lizzie. 'Thank you,' he said.

'Please,' said Lizzie. 'Please let me take it back.'

'When it's empty,' said Grandpa, 'I'll let you take the empty bottle back.'

Lizzie decided to give up, for the moment, and settle back and enjoy the afternoon on the river.

*   *   *

'It was just lovely,' she told her mother at tea time.

'I got a swan's feather, and there was a moorhen with six chicks, and they were lovely . . .'

'Sssh,' said her mother. 'There's no need to shout.'

'I wasn't,' said Lizzie. 'And Grandpa got stuck on the pole.'

'He what?'

'Oh, just a small accident,' said Grandpa. 'Not my fault.'

'It stuck in the water and the punt floated away,' said Lizzie.

Lizzie's mother tried not to laugh.

'And he was wriggling about on it, like a monkey on a stick,' screamed Lizzie.

'Sssh,' her mother warned her again.

'It was a rowing boat's fault,' explained Grandpa. 'It barged into us. I was perfectly in control until then.'

'And a fat lady in the boat shouted at Grandpa,' shouted Lizzie.

WOOF, agreed Gilbert.

'And a lady in a wide hat said he didn't orter be on the river, he really didn't orter.'

Lizzie's mother gave up trying not to laugh.

'I'm going out,' said Grandpa, with an

attempt at dignity. 'I may be late home.'

'In the end a man in another boat pushed the punt back to Grandpa and he got back on,' said Lizzie. 'So it was all right.'

'Goodbye,' called Grandpa.

SLAM!

'Oh, I think he's cross,' said Lizzie.

'No. He'll get over it,' said her mother. 'He had a wonderful day.'

'So did I,' said Lizzie.

Lizzie's mother looked serious. 'I don't know what's happening,' she said. 'What have you done?'

'Nothing.'

'Lizzie.'

'I'll sort it out,' Lizzie promised.

'But he's changing,' her mother insisted. 'Look at him just then.'

'Yes.'

'He looks younger than your father. I think he is younger than your father.'

Lizzie had not liked to admit this, but it was true. Grandpa looked at least fifteen years younger at tea time than he had at breakfast time.

'I can make it all right. I promise.'

'If only he could be himself again,' said her mother.

'But he was dying,' said Lizzie.

Her mother did not answer.

'I'll see Mrs May,' said Lizzie. 'Now.'

NINE

'I couldn't get it,' said Lizzie.

Mrs May shrugged her big shoulders. 'It doesn't matter,' she said.

'But I thought you'd be angry.'

'Angry, my dear. No need to be angry.'

'But he's still drinking it.'

Mrs May tilted her iron pot and poured a white liquid into a clear glass bottle, the same shape as the one Grandpa had in his pocket.

'He was expecting me to take it from him,' said Lizzie. 'I couldn't get near it.'

'It doesn't matter,' said Mrs May. 'Not now. Doesn't matter whether he keeps drinking it or not.'

'But he's getting younger,' said Lizzie. 'All the time. How old will he be tomorrow?'

'Ah,' said Mrs May. 'Now there's a question. All I know is, it won't stop now, whether he drinks any more or not. It won't stop.'

'But why?' asked Lizzie.

'Because,' said Mrs May, 'nothing ever stops.' She poured the last of the white liquid into the clear bottle. It was something like milk, yet not quite. There was a silver light dancing through it, making it sparkle. 'It doesn't make any difference whether you go forwards or backwards, you've got to keep on travelling.'

'But where to?' asked Lizzie. 'Where's he travelling to?'

'Oh, that's easy,' said Mrs May. 'He's travelling backwards. He's been to all these places before. The exciting thing is to travel forwards. That's what we're made for. We never know then where we're going. That really is exciting.'

'I don't understand,' complained Lizzie.

'Never mind,' said Mrs May. 'The potion has done its work. It's set him off in the other direction.' She waddled round the big kitchen table and sat down. 'I didn't mean it to. I just wanted to stop him for a few weeks, a few months, just till you had time to get used to what was going to happen to him. But you gave him the bottle, and he drank too much. And now, he's travelling backwards.'

'You said that already,' said Lizzie.

'Did I? Yes, I suppose I did.'

Lizzie stood very close to Mrs May and looked at her.

'I want it to stop,' she said. 'I want it like it was.'

Mrs May put a strong arm round her small shoulders. 'Do you?' she said, as though talking to herself. 'I thought you would.' She smoothed Lizzie's hair. 'Let me know what happens. Bring him here whenever you want. I'm not in the least angry, with you or with him. It's my fault.'

Gilbert licked Lizzie's hand.

'Thank you,' said Lizzie. 'And I am sorry.'

'Get away with you,' said Mrs May. 'Let me know what happens.'

Lizzie started to leave.

'By the way,' said Mrs May.

'Yes?'

'Has it been good? Having him like this for a few days?'

'Oh, yes.'

'Good.'

'Thank you.'

'Oh, don't thank me. But . . .'

'Yes?'

'You might just have a bit more fun before it's all over.'

*   *   *

Lizzie was fast asleep.

CRASH! CLANG!

WOOF.

'Errr?' she groaned.

WOOF.

'Shut up, Gilbert,' a voice shouted. 'Sssh. It'sh late.'

CLASH!

WOOF.

'Sssshh. Hic.' Then a giggle. 'That'sh a dushtbin. Here, let'sh pick it up.'

CLANK.

WOOF.

'Ooopsh.'

CRASH!

'Better leave it alone. Get to bed, eh?'

WOOF.

'Ssshhh.'

All went quiet outside.

Lizzie went back to sleep.

*   *   *

'Breakfast time!' Lizzie's mother called up the stairs. 'Stir yourself, Lizzie. You'll be late for school.'

Lizzie crawled out of bed and scratched her head, trying to remember what had woken her in the night. She peered out of her curtains and saw that the dustbin had fallen over and all the rubbish was strewn around.

'Ohhhh.'

Lizzie listened.

'Oooohhh.'

Grandpa was groaning.

He was ill again! He was dying. Mrs May had said it would all stop. It was too late to worry about the bottle. Lizzie ran out of her room.

'Mum! Mum! Quickly! Grandpa's ill!'

Lizzie's mother ran up the stairs two at a time.

'Where? Why? What's the matter?'

'Listen.'

'Oohhhh.'

Lizzie scraped the sleeve of her

pyjamas across her eyes.

'It's my fault,' she said. 'I took him out. He wasn't well enough and I went out with him.'

'It's all right,' said her mother. 'He was very late home last night, and you didn't take him out then, did you?'

'No.'

'And he was all right last night. At least—I didn't see him, but he called goodnight to me when he came in. I was in bed.'

'Ooohhhhhhhhhh.'

'We'd better see,' said Lizzie, but she did not dare to look when her mother opened the bedroom door.

'Ooooohhhhhh,' groaned Grandpa.

'Oh!' said Lizzie's mother.

Lizzie peeped through her fingers.

Grandpa wasn't there.

'What's all this?' snapped Lizzie's mother.

'Ooooohhh,' groaned the boy in the bed.

'Where's Grandpa?' said Lizzie.

'Hello, Lizzie,' said the boy. 'Ooohh, I've got a terrible headache.'

'I should think so, the amount you

drank last night,' said Lizzie's mother.

'Grandpa?' said Lizzie, drawing close to him.

'Is it you?'

' 'Course it's me,' said the boy. 'Who else would it be? Oohhh. I'm thirsty.'

WOOF.

Gilbert liked meeting new people.

'Ooohhh, be quiet, you stupid dog,' said the boy.

Gilbert sulked.

'You'd better come downstairs, both of you,' said Lizzie's mother. 'And we'll sort this out.'

The boy reached down into the cupboard by the bed and took a big swig from a bottle. He coughed violently, drank again, and gasped.

'Ah,' he said. 'That's better.' He shook himself. 'Cor. That's a bit of good.' He moved his head, experimentally. 'Gone,' he said. 'Headache's all gone.'

WOOF.

'Hello, Gilbert. Come to Grandpa.'

Gilbert leaped up on to the bed and licked the boy's face.

'Up you get, Jack,' said Lizzie's mother. 'Breakfast.'

The boy looked very silly when he stood up. His nightshirt flapped around him like a tent.

'Ha ha,' he said. 'What's going on here? I'm in giant's clothes.'

He looked up at Lizzie's mother. 'And you've grown,' he said in surprise. 'And you, young Lizzie.'

'We'll talk about it downstairs,' said Lizzie's mother.

'I'm a boy!' shouted Grandpa. 'I am, aren't I? I'm a boy again.'

'It rather looks like it,' agreed Lizzie's mother.

'But I can't be. I don't want to be.'

'Get dressed and come down,' she said.

'How?'

'What?'

'How? How can I get dressed? I've got no clothes.'

He looked so funny in his perplexity that Lizzie rolled on the bed and laughed.

'Stop that,' he said.

WOOF.

'I've got some clothes,' she offered.

'Can't wear a girl's clothes,' said

110

Grandpa.

'That's a good idea,' said Lizzie's mother.

'No! Won't wear a girl's clothes. Won't wear frocks. Don't be stupid,' said Grandpa.

'Here,' said Lizzie's mother. She found a pair of jeans, a sweatshirt and some trainers. 'These should do.'

'All right,' Grandpa grumbled.

'Put them on and let's have a look at you,' she said.

'Not while you're here. Wait outside.'

'We'll see you downstairs,' she said. 'Come on, Lizzie.'

WOOF.

Grandpa looked all right in Lizzie's clothes.

'That's fine,' said Lizzie's mother.

'Got any more toast?' he asked. 'And some baked beans.'

'No, eat up what you've got.'

'I'm going out today,' he said.

'You're going to school.'

'What?'

'What?' repeated Lizzie.

'You heard me. You're going to school.'

'I'm too old to go to school.'

'Not from where I'm looking you aren't.'

'I can't go.'

'You can't go out on your own. It isn't safe.'

'Well . . .'

'And I'm not having you here getting under my feet all day.'

'But . . .'

'No buts. Here's your packed lunch. And here's yours, Lizzie.'

'Thank you.'

'Thank you.'

'I'll 'phone the school and tell them you're staying with us. It's all I can do for the time being. We'll say you're a relation of Lizzie's.'

'I am a relation of Lizzie's,' said Grandpa.

'I'm not telling them you're her grandpa,' said Lizzie's mother. 'They'll think I'm mad.'

Grandpa went out, rather unwillingly, with Lizzie.

'And I'm not sure that they wouldn't be right,' Lizzie's mother said to herself as she watched them shut the door.

'Perhaps I am mad.'

WOOF, Gilbert agreed.

'We'll go in Mabel,' said Grandpa.

'Grandpa,' Lizzie began to object. 'We can't.'

'Oh, yes, we can,' said Grandpa, taking the car keys out of his pocket. 'And you'd better start calling me Jack, or people will look.'

He opened Mabel's door and climbed in.

'I'm not coming with you,' said Lizzie.

PARP PARP!

'Get in.'

'No!'

GRARRRGH, roared the engine.

PARP!

'Good old Mabel. Starts first time. Get in, Lizzie.'

'You can't drive.'

'The pedals are a bit far away,' agreed Grandpa waving his feet in the air and trying to reach them. 'We'll do our best. Get in.'

PARP!

'Now then. Now then. Now then. What's all this, then?'

'Oh, crumbs,' groaned Lizzie.

'You can't sit there, sonny,' said the policeman, kindly. 'You'll cause an accident.'

'Please mind your own business, my good man,' said Grandpa.

'Now then.' The friendly look disappeared from the policeman's red face. 'Now then, laddie. That's enough of that.'

'That's quite enough from you,' said Grandpa. 'Mind your own business.'

'Grandpa,' whispered Lizzie. 'Don't talk to him like that.'

The policeman's ears went as red as his face.

'Right,' he said. 'You've asked for it. Out you get, laddie. Double quick.'

He pulled open the door and jerked Grandpa's shoulder.

'Ow,' yelled Grandpa. 'Leave me alone. Gerroff.'

'I'm sorry, Constable,' said Lizzie. 'He was only joking. He'll stay out, now. Won't you, Gran . . . Jack?'

The policeman reached in and took the keys out of Mabel. She fell silent.

'Give them here,' demanded Grandpa.

'Now then,' said the policeman. His neck was now as red as his ears and face.

'Sorry,' said Grandpa, sullenly, scuffing his shoe on the pavement.

'I'll look after these,' said the policeman, 'until your mum or dad comes to the station for them. All right?'

'Now just you . . .' began Grandpa.

'That's fine,' said Lizzie. 'We'll tell them.'

'Yes,' said the policeman. 'And I'll have something to tell them, too. Letting you start the car up indeed. Humph.'

Grandpa scowled at the policeman's back.

'Come on,' said Lizzie. 'We'll be late for school.'

'All right,' said Grandpa.

'And you will be good at school, won't you?' she begged.

Grandpa grinned. 'I'm looking forward to going back to school,' he said. 'There's a couple of things I want to do.'

'Oh, no,' said Lizzie.

TEN

Grandpa grabbed a stick from the pavement and ran to school, banging it against fences, thumping it on gates, and rattling it along the railings by the playground. PLINK. PLINK. PLINK. PLINK. PLINK. PLINK. PLINK. PLINK. PLINK. PLINK. PLINK. PLINK. PLINK. PLINK. PLINK. PLINK. PLINK. PLINK. PLINK.

'Stop that, you boy,' thundered out a deep voice.

'Yaaaah!' answered Grandpa.

'You boy!' bellowed the voice. 'Come here, at once.'

'Shush, Grandpa,' said Lizzie. 'That's Mr Murdwood.'

'Who's he?' demanded Grandpa.

'He's a terror,' said Lizzie. 'Don't cheek him.'

They trotted towards the teacher.

'You, boy!'

'What, me?' said Grandpa, casually.

'Yes, boy. You, boy. What do you think you mean?'

116

'Come again,' said Grandpa.

Mr Murdwood's mouth dropped open. No one ever spoke to him like this.

'Do you know who I am, boy?' he demanded.

'No.'

This was the wrong answer. Grandpa was supposed to say. 'Yes, sir. Sorry, sir. Mr Murdwood, sir.' Then Mr Murdwood could really get going and give him a telling off he'd never forget. That was what Mr Murdwood often did to children. 'I gave him a telling off he'll never forget,' Mr Murdwood used to say to the other teachers.

'Please, sir,' said Lizzie. 'He doesn't come to this school, sir. So he really doesn't know who you are. Really and truly.'

The other children in the playground were taking a friendly interest in all this.

'Well, you listen to me, er, you, what's your name?'

'Mr Blake,' said Grandpa.

The children sniggered.

Mr Murdwood clenched his jaws.

'Don't you be clever to me, boy,' he said. 'What's your name?'

'I've told you,' said Grandpa, 'Mr Blake. What's yours?'

'Right, that's it,' said Mr Murdwood. 'You're coming with me.' He took Grandpa by the scruff of his neck and marched him off. There was a small cheer from the onlookers. 'And you, girl,' he said to Lizzie. 'Lizzie, isn't it? Miss Goodings' class. You come with me, as well.'

'Oh, no,' groaned Lizzie, and she hung her head in shame and followed.

'Gerroff,' Grandpa protested.

'Oh, please,' whispered Lizzie to herself. 'Please be quiet, Grandpa.'

The Headmaster was very surprised to see Mr Murdwood burst into his study with a strange boy in his hand and a shy little girl peeping round the door.

'Lizzie, isn't it?' he asked. 'How are you?'

'Very well, thank you,' said Lizzie.

'Well, I'm dashed well not,' said Grandpa. 'Tell this fellow to let go of me.'

118

'You see,' said Mr Murdwood.

'No, I don't really,' admitted the Headmaster. 'No, I don't see.'

'I'll have the law on him,' said Grandpa. And he aimed a kick at Mr Murdwood's leg.

'Ow.'

'Gotchya!' said Grandpa. 'Only had to wait till you were standing still.'

'Grandpa,' said Lizzie. 'You mustn't.'

The Headmaster looked puzzled.

'Er, no,' he agreed. 'You mustn't do that.'

'You see,' said Mr Murdwood again. He was rubbing his leg and hopping.

'No,' said the Headmaster again. 'I still don't see. Do you see, Lizzie?'

And Lizzie tried to convince the Headmaster that Grandpa (or rather Jack Blake, her relative who was staying with her) had got on the wrong side of Mr Murdwood, and as a lot of people were always getting on the wrong side of Mr Murdwood the Headmaster was soon satisfied.

'But if you're coming to this school while you stay with Lizzie you'd better learn to be more polite to the teachers,'

119

he told Grandpa, quite sternly.

'He seems a decent old cove,' said Grandpa as he and Lizzie went to their classroom.

'Please try to behave,' Lizzie said.

'Did you see his face when I kicked him?' Grandpa giggled.

Lizzie giggled as well.

'And the Headmaster's face, when you called me Grandpa?'

'Here we are,' said Lizzie. 'And please be nice to Miss Goodings.'

'All right,' agreed Grandpa.

Lizzie heaved a sigh of relief.

'If she's nice to me,' he added.

Miss Goodings settled Grandpa in cheerfully and made him sit on the other side of the room from Lizzie.

'We're learning about the Second World War,' she explained. 'And we were just thinking about how people felt when the cities were bombed.'

'Frightened,' said Lennie.

'No,' said Jo, 'they were brave. Didn't mind a few bombs.'

'They had shelters,' said Graham.

'And they hid in them, so they must have been frightened,' said Lennie. He beamed round in victory.

'Don't have to be frightened to go in a bomb shelter,' said Lizzie.

'Be stupid if you didn't go in,' said Graham.

'No,' said Lennie. 'Think about it. You'd be stupid if you weren't frightened. I mean, bombs dropping and blowing everything up. You'd have to be frightened.'

'BOOM!' said Graham.

Anna stretched out her arms. 'Nyyyyaaaaaahhhh,' she whined.

'BOOOM!' said Graham again.

'Stop,' said Miss Goodings, with a smile. 'That's enough.'

'It wasn't like that,' said Grandpa quietly.

'BOOM!' said Graham, although with less conviction than before. Miss Goodings gave him her be quiet look.

'What was that, Jack?' she said, encouragingly.

'Not like that,' he said again. 'Not here, at any rate.'

'No?' she prompted him.

'Most of the bombs didn't make a noise, not much of one. They didn't

121

explode.'

Graham laughed. 'That's what they do,' he said. 'That's what bombs are for.' And he added a final, very quiet, 'boom'.

'Not these,' said Jack. His small, young face was sad. 'They burst open, quietly, then they threw fire out. That's what they were. Incendiaries. Fire bombs.'

The class was as silent as snow.

'They dropped them all over the city. They rolled off the roofs. They smashed through tiles. They spilled open and poured their fire all over the city. Houses. Shops. Hospitals. Cinemas. Everywhere. You could smell the meat cooking in the butchers' shops.'

'Yum, yum,' said Anna.

'Ssh,' said Miss Goodings.

'Was it only meat?' asked Lennie.

Grandpa ignored him.

'And the churches,' he said. 'They were all on fire. Everywhere. It was the middle of the night, and there was a moon, very bright, full and clear. And the light from the flames. It was as bright as day. And the planes kept on coming, more and more of them with the bombs. People were running for cover and there was no cover. Some were trapped in their houses and couldn't get out while the flames swallowed whole streets.'

'Why?' said Graham. 'Why did they do it?'

'The factories,' said Grandpa. 'They wanted to destroy the factories. They were making our aeroplanes, cars, everything for the war. They wanted to knock them out. But they did the whole city as well, not just the factories. The dogs went mad with it all. Buildings crashed down as the fire weakened them. And the heat, and the panic. Dogs frighten easily. But the people weren't that frightened,' he said to Lennie. 'Not really. There didn't seem to be time.'

Lennie, whose mouth was wide open, nodded.

'But the next morning,' said Grandpa, slowly and quietly, 'you looked for your friends, and they were gone. The smell of smoke was still there, and the ashes beneath your feet wherever you went. And the glow beneath the cold grey broke out if you kicked it. The fire was still there. But the people were gone. Tommy Ellis, Stan French, Harry Eyres. All gone. All dead. In their twenties, thirties. Young men. They stayed to help. Tried to fight the fires. But it was no good. There were too many bombs, not enough fire engines. Not enough water.

'And families broken up. Children: Tony James was seven; Timmy Smail was twelve; Hilda Russell, she was nine. And Patty Blake, my little sister, fifteen, dead.'

Grandpa stopped and stared at the rest of the class.

'So you weren't frightened,' he said. 'Not at the time. Not till later. Much later.'

Suddenly, Lennie laughed.

Lizzie held her breath.

Miss Goodings glared at Lennie. 'Thank you, Jack,' she said. 'You told that beautifully. It must have been just like that. You might almost have been there.'

'Oh,' said Grandpa, pushing back his chair and standing up, 'I was. I was there. But I think it's time I left, now. I ought to be on my way.'

ELEVEN

Lizzie ran out of the classroom after Grandpa.

'Stop! Stop!'

Grandpa sprinted across the playground, through the gate and off.

Lizzie reached the gate and looked down the road. Grandpa's feet disappeared round the corner.

'Now then,' thundered a voice through a window. 'What's going on here?' Mr Murdwood glared down at Lizzie. 'Out of your classroom. You'll be in trouble again, my girl. Who said you could be out here?'

'I did,' said Miss Goodings.

Lizzie turned round gratefully.

'But I think you'd better come back in now, don't you?' And she placed her hand on Lizzie's back and gently steered her back inside.

'Do you want to tell me about it?' she asked.

'No.'

'All right.'

Lizzie smiled gratefully at her.

'But I think Jack's used to going out on his own, isn't he?'

Lizzie agreed.

'So we don't have to ring your mum?'

'No,' said Lizzie.

'Right, then,' said Miss Goodings. 'I'm sure I don't understand, but I'll do what you say.'

'Thank you,' said Lizzie.

'Is Jack who I think he is?' she asked.

'I expect so,' said Lizzie.

'Well,' said Miss Goodings. 'How exciting.'

'Yes,' said Lizzie. 'I'll go and look for him at lunch time. I'm still very worried.'

'Come on,' said Miss Goodings. 'Let's keep you busy till then. That's the best thing to do.'

And it was.

*   *   *

Lizzie hoped that Grandpa would be waiting for her at the gate at lunch time, but he wasn't.

She crept into the house and peered

into his bedroom, but he wasn't there. She could hear her mother downstairs in the study so she took special care to be quiet. The floor creaked beneath her feet, but Lizzie walked right over to his bed and looked in the little cupboard next to it.

It was there. The little green bottle was in there. Lizzie took it eagerly and stuffed it up her jumper.

She was so excited she nearly tripped down the stairs and gave herself away, but she managed to recover her balance and get out of the house.

WOOF, said Gilbert happily when he spotted her in the garden.

'Ssshh,' she warned him.

WOOF, he said again, louder.

They ran off together.

Lizzie's mother put her head out of the window and looked around.

'Funny,' she said. 'I thought I heard –'

WOOF? asked Gilbert when they were clear of the house.

'Mrs May's,' answered Lizzie. 'I've got the bottle.'

She was running with her arms folded over her jumper and it was difficult, so she stopped and took out the bottle.

'I wonder,' she said.

She pulled the cork.

The wonderful aroma of fields and woods and meadows swirled around her, making her head spin.

She peeped inside. The bottle was as full now as it had been the day Mrs May had given it to her.

'I wonder,' she said. 'It smells so wonderful. What can it taste like?'

She raised the bottle to her lips.

WOOF, Gilbert warned her.

'Just a sip,' she explained. 'It wouldn't do any harm.'

WOOF. Gilbert beat an unhappy tail on the pavement.

Lizzie held the bottle near to her lips.

'I might just be a week younger,' she said. 'If I just touched the tip of my tongue against it, just to taste it.'

Gilbert jumped up and tried to push the bottle away from her mouth.

'Careful!' shouted Lizzie. 'I'm dropping it.'

The bottle tumbled from her hands. Lizzie dived, felt it in her fingers, it slipped again and she swooped down to grab it before it could smash on the paving stones.

'Get away,' she warned. 'Stop. It's slipping. You'll break it.'

She juggled it around. It was slippery and it wriggled. She almost lost it.

WOOF.

'Stop!'

Grab.

'There. Got it.'

'Hello.'

Lizzie looked round.

'Hello,' she said.

The little boy was only about three or four. He wore clothes that were laughably too big for him, jeans and a sweatshirt. He took a step nearer to her and his trainers fell off his feet and stayed where they were.

'You nearly broke that,' he said.

'I caught it, though,' Lizzie told him in a cross voice. She did not like to be told off by such a small child.

'Shall I look after it for you?' he asked.

'You,' she laughed. 'How could you? You're too little.'

The little boy looked at himself, then

he raised his head and looked up at Lizzie.

'I know I'm little,' he agreed, 'but I'd like the bottle. So that I can take it back to the lady.'

'What?' said Lizzie.

'I'm frightened,' he said. His eyes were wet. 'Please may we take the bottle back?'

Lizzie stared at him.

'Grandpa?' she asked.

'Yes,' said the little boy. 'Come on, Lizzie. Let's have the bottle.'

*   *   *

Lizzie turned the old-fashioned latch and stuck her head round the door.

'Mrs May!' she called out. 'It's Lizzie.'

Gilbert woofed to show that he was there too.

'Come on in. Come on in,' her voice sang out.

The house was still and peaceful.

'Hello, Jack,' she said.

Grandpa nodded to her. Lizzie had turned up the legs of his jeans and the sleeves of his sweatshirt, but there had been nothing she could do about the big trainers so his feet were bare on the red tiles of the kitchen floor.

Mrs May smiled at him. 'Have you brought something for me?' she asked.

Grandpa gave her the bottle.

Mrs May held it up to the light to see if it was still full. Lizzie watched. The light from the window searched through the dark glass of the bottle. Inside, Lizzie seemed to see trees and flowers, the swaying of branches and the clinging of tendrils. The liquid shimmered and moved.

'Ah,' said Mrs May. 'That's all right, then.'

And she put the bottle back into her cupboard.

'Now then,' she said.

She sat down in her wooden chair with the curly arms and she gestured to Grandpa. He went over to her, scrambled up and sat himself down on her wide lap. Lizzie looked at them in wonder. Grandpa slipped his thumb into his mouth and snuggled up to Mrs May who cuddled him and smoothed his hair.

'What are we going to do?' she asked him quietly.

Grandpa pulled out a wet thumb.

'I want to go back,' he said.

'Do you? Do you really?'

'Yes.'

'And what about you, Lizzie?'

'It's nothing to do with her,' said Grandpa. 'It's my life. I can choose.'

'Not really,' said Mrs May. 'It was Lizzie who came and asked for the potion. It ought to be Lizzie who asks for it to stop.'

'But I can't carry on like this,' said Grandpa. 'I'll be a baby soon. And then . . .'

'Yes,' said Mrs May. 'And then.'

'What can we do?' asked Lizzie.

'We can carry on,' said Mrs May, 'and see what happens. Or we can change it all back again.'

'Exactly like it was?' asked Lizzie.

'Exactly,' warned Mrs May.

'Or?' asked Lizzie.

'I was hoping you wouldn't ask that,' said Mrs May.

'Or?' said Lizzie.

133

'Or, I suppose,' said Mrs May, 'we could decide on an age and keep him at it.'

'For ever?' asked Lizzie.

'As good as,' said Mrs May.

'Here,' objected Grandpa. 'Stop talking about me as if I wasn't here.'

'That's the most difficult one,' said Mrs May to Lizzie. 'But we could do it.'

'So he'd be Grandpa all the time?'

'All the time,' agreed Mrs May.

'But not poorly?'

'No, not poorly. But old, if you like. The way you remember him. The way you wanted him. The way he would have stayed if only he'd brought the bottle back after one dose.'

Grandpa shuffled about uncomfortably.

'That's what I'd like best,' said Lizzie.

'No you don't,' said Grandpa. 'You turn me round and set me going again.'

Mrs May looked at Lizzie and waited.

Gilbert licked Lizzie's hand.

Lizzie looked at Grandpa. Already his little hands were disappearing up the rolled up sleeves of the sweatshirt. He was getting younger faster and faster.

'I want you for ever,' she said to him. 'I want you back the way you were, that first day. The day we went to the seaside and met Laurie.'

'I've had enough of seasides,' said Grandpa in a small voice, 'and crabs and motor cars and schools. What about Tommy Ellis, and Stan French?'

Lizzie dragged her sleeve across her eyes.

'And Tony James,' he said.

'And Timmy Smail,' said Mrs May. 'And Hilda Russell.'

'That's right,' said Grandpa. 'And Patty,' he added.

'And Patty,' agreed Mrs May.

'It's about time,' said Grandpa.

'What do you think?' Mrs May asked Lizzie.

'I think so,' said Lizzie, very, very quietly.

Mrs May produced the clear glass bottle with the white liquid in it. The flashes of silver that burst from it were brighter even than the clear sunlight falling in through the window.

'As much as you like,' she said to

135

Grandpa. 'It doesn't matter.'

Grandpa drank deeply, then gasped.

'It's wonderful,' he said. 'Even better than the green one. Can I?'

'Of course,' she said. 'As much as you want.'

Grandpa drank again.

'Thank you,' he said.

Mrs May bent over and kissed his cheek. He smiled up at her.

'Come along,' he said to Lizzie.

Lizzie took his small hand in hers and led him home.

'What will happen?' she asked him.

TWELVE

Grandpa was very tired when Lizzie arrived home so he had a hot bath and went straight to bed. Lizzie peeped in at him when she was ready for bed. His brown hair spread out on the pillow. His small pink cheeks were pulled in slightly as he sucked at his thumb. He looked so lovely and restful and contented that Lizzie wanted to stroke him like a puppy.

'Goodnight, Grandpa,' she said. And she kissed him.

Lizzie thought she would sleep badly, worrying about Grandpa, but as soon as she turned over in bed she stepped into a happy dream.

Aeroplanes circled a city in a full moon. They spilled bombs into the soft darkness. All around her fires sprang up, but she was not afraid and no heat from them scorched her.

'Hello,' said Grandpa.

'Hello,' said Lizzie, and she slipped her hand into his. He was young again,

137

not a child or a boy, but a man, just. They walked together through the burning city. Lizzie could smell the meat cooking in the butchers' shops.

Some people ran around, busy, frightened, important, or just confused. They trained hoses onto flames, but as soon as one fire was out ten others sprang up. They ran for cover, where there was no cover. They cursed the moon for being so bright and the planes for being so dark.

Others, many others, ignored what was happening and joined hands with one another and set off, all in the same direction. They stepped calmly through the rubble and the embers. Young men scooped children into their arms and carried them away. Young women took the hands of the older ones and helped them loose from the things that held them back. Old people stood confidently and made their way with the rest.

'There,' said Grandpa, pointing. 'There she is.'

'Who?' asked Lizzie.

'Over here!' called Grandpa.

A girl, fourteen, fifteen years old perhaps, turned and waited.

'Here!' Grandpa shouted again, and he waved.

The girl waved back.

'Goodbye,' he said to Lizzie.

'I'm coming with you,' she said.

'Not yet,' said Grandpa. 'Plenty of time.'

He let go of her hand, stooped to kiss her and walked towards the girl.

'Wait!' called Lizzie.

She tried to run after him, but she tripped and twisted her ankle.

'Wait!'

Grandpa took the girl's hand, they smiled at each other, then, together, they waved to Lizzie and walked off with the others.

'Stop!' called Lizzie. 'You can't leave me.'

She looked up into the dark sky. The bombs were falling, faster and thicker. They jolted into the ground and burst open with flowers of fire. Lizzie could feel the heat on her cheeks now, but she could not move from where she had fallen.

'Wait!' she called. 'Grandpa, help!'

She started to sob and the noise inside her grew louder and louder, drowning the drone of the aeroplanes until all she could hear was the sound of crying.

The light from the fires bloomed out, hurting her eyes. She screwed her hands into fists and rubbed her eyes. The noise of the sobbing came louder.

Lizzie uncovered her eyes and saw that the curtain had blown aside from her window and that the early sun was piercing into her face.

'Ugh?' she grunted.

The sobbing, quieter now, but persistent still, caught her ears and she slipped out of bed to look for it.

'All right, Lizzie,' said her father, taking her into his arms and lifting her up as she stepped on to the landing. 'It's all right.'

His eyes were red, but the sobbing still came through to her.

'What's happening?'

'It's all right, Lizzie,' he said again.

'All right,' she agreed. 'But what's happening?'

Grandpa's door opened and her mother stepped out. She closed it quickly behind her, caught her breath and blew her nose. The sobbing had stopped now.

'Can I see Grandpa?' Lizzie asked.

'I don't think you should,' said her mother.

When Crawly and Uncle George and Aunty Nell and Sniffy Clara had been there Lizzie had known that she never wanted to see Grandpa when he was dead. Now it was different.

They did not try to stop her when she opened the door and stepped through.

*   *   *

'Well,' said Mrs May. 'That's it then.'

'Thank you for coming,' said Lizzie's mother.

'You'll come home for some tea?' asked her father.

'That would be nice,' said Mrs May.

'All right, Lizzie?' her father asked.

Lizzie smiled at them all. She knew that if she tried to speak she would start to cry again.

Uncle George and Aunty Nell and Crawly and Aunty Clara looked out through the windows of the big black car at them.

'She's all right,' said Mrs May.

Uncle George looked at his watch.

'We'd better get in,' said Lizzie's mother.

Lizzie looked across at the men who were shovelling the crumbly earth.

'Can't I stay a bit?' she asked with a trembling voice.

'You ought to come back,' said her mother. She put her arm round Lizzie. 'It's over now. Time to go home.'

'Let's get in the car,' said Lizzie's father.

'I can't get back in that thing,' said Mrs May. 'It'll ruin my legs. Let me walk home with Lizzie.'

They stood together watching the car disappear.

WOOF.

Gilbert jumped out from behind a gravestone.

'Oh, good boy,' said Lizzie in more her usual voice. 'Good boy. You came after all.'

WOOF.

Gilbert ran over to the new grave. Lizzie and Mrs May followed.

The familiar, intense smell of trees and grass and growth drifted up when the gravediggers sliced their spades into the loose earth and replaced it.

'I thought he would still be a boy,' said Lizzie.

'No,' said Mrs May.

'But he looked the way he always had. Grey hair, wrinkles, those funny brown blotches on the back of his hands.'

The gravediggers smoothed the top of the fresh grave, stood back, nodded in satisfaction, shouldered their spades and walked off.

'I stroked his hair,' said Lizzie. 'Then I kissed his cheek and said goodbye.'

'Was it worth it?' asked Mrs May.

'Oh, yes,' said Lizzie. 'It was worth it. I'll never forget the day at the seaside.'

WOOF, agreed Gilbert.

'And on the river,' said Lizzie. 'He was so funny, hanging on to that pole.'

Mrs May pulled a small branch from a tree. It fought to stay where it was.

The wood was damp and springy and would not snap. Mrs May had to twist it to break it off. She dropped it on Grandpa's grave.

'Goodbye,' she said.

She took Lizzie's hand and led her away.

'Not too fast,' she said. 'I'll get too hot in this sun.'

'But he couldn't have stayed,' said Lizzie.

'No,' agreed Mrs May.

'I wish we didn't have to go back,' said Lizzie. 'I don't want to talk to them.'

'Chin up,' said Mrs May. 'They'll soon be gone.'

*   *   *

'I really don't know what got . . .' said Aunty Nell.

'. . . into him,' said Uncle George. 'A man of his age, running around . . .'

'. . . like a teenager,' said Aunty Nell.

'Sniff.'

'And,' she went on, 'he wasn't a well . . .'

'. . . man,' said Uncle George. 'It could have been the . . .'

'. . . death of him,' said Aunty Nell.

'No!' said Lizzie sharply. 'You mustn't say that. I'll . . .'

But before she could say what she would do she was interrupted.

RAT-A-TAT-TAT!

Lizzie's mother let a footman in with a huge wicker basket.

'Is Mr Doolan here yet?' he asked.

'There's no Mr Doolan,' said her father.

The footman breathed in deeply and made his tiger waistcoat swell with dignity. 'Then I must wait until he arrives,' he said.

'No,' said Uncle George, 'there isn't a . . .'

'. . . Mr Doolan,' said Aunty Nell. 'So you'd . . .'

The footman gave them both a look of complete disdain and stayed where he was.

'. . . better go, now,' said Uncle George. 'You can't stay here. This is a . . .'

'Sniff.'

RAT-A-TAT-TAT!

'Funeral,' said Aunty Clara.

'Who on earth can that be?' asked Lizzie's father.

'Oh, you're all here,' said Mr Doolan. 'Sorry if I'm a bit late.'

He was tall and thin and wore a black jacket and stripy trousers.

'Good. You've brought the hamper, Flannell,' he said to the footman. The footman stood to attention.

'The late Mr Jack Blake has asked me to read his will and to dispense the bequests immediately,' said Mr Doolan.

Uncle George and Aunty Nell and Aunty Clara suddenly lost their hostile faces and became attentive.

'We're terribly . . .'

'. . . sorry. We . . .'

'. . . didn't realise that you . . .'

'. . . were a solicitor. Won't you have a . . .'

'. . . ham sandwich?' said Aunty Nell.

'. . . seat,' glowered Uncle George.

'Very kind,' said Mr Doolan. 'No time, I'm afraid. Must get on with . . .'

'. . . the business,' said Uncle George

and Aunty Clara together, very eagerly.

'He knew I wanted that clock,' said Aunty Nell.

'And he promised me his house,' said Uncle George. 'I had it in a letter somewhere, but I might have lost it. But he did promise.'

'Hrrummph,' Mr Doolan cleared his throat. 'Mr Blake's wishes are quite clearly stated in his will,' he said.

'But he might have changed . . .'

'. . . his mind. He was . . .'

'. . . ill.'

'Mr Blake saw me only a matter of a few days ago,' said Mr Doolan. 'And I was delighted to see how well he looked. So well, in fact, that I am surprised as well as saddened to be executing his last wishes so soon after he expressed them.'

'Get on with it,' whispered Crawly.

Lizzie pinched him very hard. 'You beast,' she said. 'You don't care about Grandpa, any of you. You're only here for what you can get.'

'Waaaah!' complained Crawly. 'She pinched me.'

'Oh, be . . .'

'. . . quiet.'

'Sniff.'

'The document is dated and witnessed and reads as follows,' said Mr Doolan. '"I, Jack Blake, being of sound mind, make arrangement for the distribution of all my . . ."'

'Can't you just . . .'

'. . . tell us? Do you have to . . .'

'. . . read it all?'

Mr Doolan wriggled his thin shoulders and smiled to himself, a smile with no warmth or humour. 'Mr Blake did warn me that there might be a desire to learn the contents of the will quickly and he gave me his verbal permission to abandon the reading and proceed immediately to the distribution.'

'Yes,' said the others.

'The hamper, Flannell,' said Mr Doolan.

Flannell threw open the lid of the hamper with a flourish and drew out a huge bottle of champagne.

POP.

He held the bottle expertly so that not a drop of the foaming wine spilled out, then filled glasses swiftly and handed them round.

Uncle George's eyes sparkled like the wine.

'This is generous,' he said, 'very . . .'

'. . . wasteful,' finished Aunty Nell. 'This money could have been saved . . .'

'I think Grandpa could do what he wanted with his own money,' said Lizzie's father. He raised his glass. 'Bung ho, Grandpa.'

'Sniff.'

Fizzy orange appeared and was served to Lizzie and Crawly.

'Do we all have a drink?' asked Mr Doolan.

WOOF, said Gilbert.

Flannell produced an enormous bone with a red ribbon round it.

WOOF, said Gilbert gratefully.

'Then,' said Mr Doolan, 'to the bequests.'

The aunts and uncle and Crawly leaned forward. Lizzie's mother and father held hands and looked out of the window, sipping their champagne.

Flannell produced a parcel labelled: 'George and Nell, to help you through to the end' and another, smaller one, labelled: 'Clara, to look after all your needs' and a third, labelled: 'Crawly, to help you to find your place in life.'

They each seized their parcel and waited.

'Any more?' demanded George.

'No,' said Mr Doolan.

They smirked.

'I don't want anything,' said Lizzie.

'It's because you upset Grandpa,' said Crawly. 'That's why he hasn't left you lot anything.'

'Hush, Crawfy,' said Uncle George. 'Don't . . .'

'. . . gloat,' said Aunty Nell. 'I'm sure they're very sorry . . .'

'. . . now, for the way they . . .'

'. . . treated Grandpa.'

'Sniff.'

Lizzie felt her heart thumping. She remembered what Grandpa had said. 'Aren't you going to open them?'

'Perhaps we . . .'

'. . . should. It's a . . .'

'. . . legacy. To see us through, with enough . . .'

'. . . money, for the rest of . . .'

'. . . our lives. All of . . .'

'. . . us.'

'Sniff.'

The relatives looked at each other in triumph, then they ripped the paper from their parcels.

'It's a . . .'

'. . . dictionary.'

'Handkerchiefs.'

'Ugh! A horrid book about insects and slugs and spiders and all sorts of creepy crawlies.'

'Hrrummph,' Mr Doolan cleared his throat. He read from the will. ' "The sealed parcels represent the total legacy to those members of my family who receive them, together with a glass of champagne or fizzy orange. The residue," ' he paused, looked over the top of his glasses at Lizzie and said to her, 'that means everything else. "All goes to Lizzie Blake, my granddaughter." That's you,' he said to Lizzie.

Gilbert licked her hand.

'What do you mean?' she said.

'Don't . . .'

'. . . shout,' said Uncle George.

'I mean,' said Mr Doolan, 'that you have inherited everything from your grandfather, except for those three presents.'

'This is . . .'

'. . . outrageous.'

'Sniff.'

'We'll fight it in . . .'

'. . . the courts. He must have been . . .'

'. . . out of his mind to . . .'

'. . . leave everything to that . . .'

'. . . that . . .'

'. . . that . . .'

'. . . that . . .'

Words failed Uncle George and Aunty Nell.

'Look it up in the dictionary,' said Lizzie's father.

'We'll get our . . .'

'. . . share. Don't you . . .'

'. . . worry. We'll get what's . . .'

'. . . coming to us,' they warned.

'But I don't want it,' said Lizzie. 'I just want . . .'

'What?' snapped Uncle George. 'What do you . . .'

'. . . want?'

'I just want Grandpa back,' began Lizzie. Then she thought and corrected herself. 'No, I don't,' she said. 'I don't want him back. I want him to be where he belongs.'

'Wherever that is,' added Mrs May, who had been sitting in silence all this time.

'Yes,' said Lizzie.

'You see,' said Aunty Nell. 'She wants him to be . . .'

'. . . dead,' said Uncle George.

'I don't see why not,' said Lizzie. 'It seems the best thing.'

There was uproar and outrage from the relatives. Lizzie's father drained his glass and said, 'Off you go, then. All of you.'

'What?'

'Sniff?'

'Where?'

'Out. The lot of you. I don't want to see you again.'

The footman plucked their glasses out of their hands, put his palms on their backs and efficiently steered them, objecting loudly, out of the house.

'That's in the will, too,' said Mr Doolan. 'They're to be pushed out as soon as you say so.'

WOOF.

'I think so, too,' agreed Mr Doolan.

Flannell's tiger waistcoat prevented the relatives from getting back into the house. They edged reluctantly down the garden path as he drove them away.

Lizzie whispered something to Mr Doolan.

'Mabel?' he said.

Lizzie nodded.

'Oh, yes, everything,' he assured her. 'It's quite clear.'

'For my very own?'

'Yes. Of course, you can't drive her yet. Not until you're older.'

Lizzie looked at her parents. 'Please,' she said.

'Marvellous idea,' agreed her father.

'Couldn't be better,' said her mother. 'Mrs May?'

'I'd love to come,' she said.

WOOF.

They were led down the path by Mr Doolan, who elbowed the relatives aside and held open Mabel's door.

PARP!

'What a . . .'

'. . . sight. It's a . . .'

'. . . disgrace.'

WOOF.

PARP!

Flannell put the huge bottle of champagne into the car with them.

GRAAAGGHH.

Mabel shuddered into life.

'Where to?' asked Lizzie's father.

'Anywhere,' said Lizzie. 'Away from that lot.'

Lizzie's mother slipped the clutch and Mabel jerked forward.

'We're off.'

They cheered and waved to the furious relatives.

'And we'll go on forever,' said Lizzie's father.

'No,' said Lizzie. 'Not forever. Just long enough. Just till it's time.'

'Time for what?' he asked.

WOOF, said Gilbert.

'Time to go,' said Lizzie.

PARP!

The grumbles and complaints of the

relatives grew fainter and fainter as they drove away, until they disappeared altogether, lost in the distance and the noise of Lizzie's laughter and her parents' cheerful voices.